The Great Timbers

The Great Timbers

The Great Timbers

The Great Timbers

By

James A. Kane

THE GREAT TIMBERS
Copyright © 2023 by Rusty Ogre Publishing

Rusty Ogre Publishing
www.rustyogrepublishing.com

All Rights Reserved.

No part of this book may be reproduced in any manner, or transmitted in any form or by any means, electronic, mechanical, photocopying, recording or otherwise, without express written permission by the author(s) and or publisher, except for the use of a brief quotation in a book review.

This book is a work of fiction.
Names, characters, places, events, organizations and incidents are either part of the author's imagination or are used fictitiously.

Any resemblance to actual persons, living or dead, or actual events is purely coincidental.

Published by Rusty Ogre Publishing
Cover Design by Erica Summers

For Renesmee

The Great Timbers

The Great Timbers

The Great Timbers

A NOTE FROM RUSTY OGRE PUBLISHING:

Even though this book was proofread thoroughly by professionals, mistakes happen. We want our readers to have the best experience possible. If you spot any spelling, grammatical, or formatting errors, please let us know so we can rectify them immediately. You can reach out to us at: Rustyogrepublishing@gmail.com

Screenshots are lovely, but if unavailable, the entire sentence, page number, and format type will suffice! We *always* appreciate your feedback.

REVIEWS:

If you could take the time to leave an honest review after you've read this book, we would greatly appreciate it. We respect your time and promise it doesn't *have* to be long and eloquent. Even a few words or a star rating will do! As a small publishing house, every review allows us to better ourselves. It also helps others determine if this book is right for them. It dramatically helps our ranking and algorithms on those platforms, even if it isn't five stars.

Want updates on any sequels or upcoming releases?

Join our mailing list at

www.rustyogrepublishing.com

THE
GREAT TIMBERS
THE
MEADOW
CAMP

THE
ROCKY
MOUNTAINS
KILGORE'S
CAVE
PLATEAU

The Great Timbers

Prologue

The Alignment

Years ago, the moon crested a wave of treetops, rising into the night sky and pushing its way past the stars. Its brilliant light shone down from above, illuminating lush woods full of towering pines and the grass-filled meadow the native animals had come to call *The Great Timbers*.

Atop a south-facing slope, a massive, full-grown Rocky Mountain elk gazed up at the smattering of brilliant, celestial bodies peppering the heavens. It loomed high and clear above his broad set of antlers, unrivaled by the hint of any man-made lights for miles.

Behind him, the leaves rustled. A yearling stepped through the crunching foliage of the meadow until they were side-by-side. The larger of the two never pried his soft brown eyes from the firmament.

"Dad, what're you doing out here," the meek yearling asked.

"See those stars over there?" With his massive antlers, the bull motioned to the vast expanse beyond the treeline.

"The tiny sparkles?"

"Yes." The father's lips curled upward into a slight smirk. "Do you see how those stars look like our antlers if you look at them just right?"

"Kind of," the yearling responded after a long pause.

"Your grandfather, Dox, once told me that when those stars align to form the image of our antlers, the wish you make upon them will come true. It doesn't happen often."

"So, if I make a wish right now," he hesitated and looked at his father with a glimmer of excitement, "it might come true?"

"So he used to say," he retorted with a blend of melancholy and dreamlike nostalgia in his voice.

"Come on, Dad," the excited yearling said, "let's do it! Let's make a wish!"

Lemuel buckled his legs and lowered himself to the tall grass beside his exhilarated son. His gaze again drifted upward as he spoke, "I wish I was younger and had the speed I once possessed. I've gotten old. I'm not as spry as I used to be. If you're lucky, you and Melvin will know what that's like one day." Lemuel chuckled.

The adolescent lay down beside his father, staring at him in adoration. "You *are* fast, Dad! You're the fastest of the whole herd by *far*."

The bull rubbed his nose on his son's budding mane in a warm display of fatherly affection. He closed his eyes and made the silent wish again in his mind. The fur-covered progeny watched his father intently and finally closed his eyes.

The father opened his eyes to see his son's eyelids clamped closed and asked, "What are you wishing for?"

The yearling's eyes sprung open. "I wish that someday… I can be like you."

The response struck the father with a wave of surprising emotion, but he did not say a word. He only lowered his head into the tall grass and smiled. They fell asleep in concave beds of bent, beige grass beneath the sparkling sea of stars in the velvet-black sky.

PART I:

The Scout

1

Mickey's beat-up pickup truck rattled down the interstate with an audible chug. His blue eyes flit to the rear-view mirror, and he watched the mesmerizing sway of the trailer behind him. The bone-white side-by-side atop it looked like skeletal remains of a tiny SUV, bobbing on red, spring shocks like a sad child on a trampoline with every dip in the road.

The large dog in the middle seat, sitting tall, leaned in to lick the side of the driver's face in an act of joyous affection.

"Ugh, Keeka!" Mickey whipped away from it, nearly smacking his head against his side window. "Notches, get your mutt off'a me. I'm driving!"

"She's not a *mutt*." Notches immediately took offense to the word as if it were absolutely blasphemous. He wrapped his spindly arm around the animal and hugged her close, brushing a tanned hand over her dense, tri-color fur.

Keeka was a beautiful wolfdog with eyes like polished, azure marbles and a dusty, crimson bandanna tied around her neck, one that partially obscured her tracking collar.

"He didn't mean it, girl." Notches rubbed both hands on the sides of her face lovingly and talked to her like an infant. "You're no mutt, are ya? *No.* You're daddy's wolfdog. I was on a waitin' list for two years to get you imported."

"You know she's illegal in most states, right?" Mickey snarled.

"You think I don't *know that*, you moron?" Notches fired back, leaning against the dashboard to stare around the dog at him.

"Wolves aren't *pets*."

"She's *half* wolf. *Utonagan*, actually."

"Half-wolf for a half-*wit*," Mickey growled, staring forward at the road, gripping the steering wheel tight.

"What did you just call me?"

"Cool it. *Both* of you." Jimmy snapped at them from the back seat, staring off into the miles of red-dirt plains stretching around them.

But Notches continued. "She's legal in Colorado."

"We're not *in* Colorado!" Mickey's blood was boiling.

"Hey, this girl's the best huntin' dog I've ever had! She was worth every *cent*, and she wasn't *cheap.*"

Keeka innocently turned her face to Mickey, panting her hot gusts of breath in his face again.

He fumed, refusing to look at her.

"I hope that dog takes off one day and don't come back." Mickey's dull blue eyes stared forward, watching a rabbit dart across the road in front of them. He never once considered braking.

"Listen, you boys better straighten up and *play nice*." Jimmy barked from the bench seat behind them. "I brought you out here to glass, not to *bicker like children*. If I wanted to hear someone whine all day, I'd go back to my ex-wife." Jimmy fought the urge to smile at his own joke.

"Which *one*?" Notches giggled, a high-pitched sound that made Mickey cringe every time he heard it. He sounded like a backwoods *hick* every time he did it.

"*Seriously*. If you two are going to fight each other this whole scout, you can drop me off back in Casper and--"

"And, *what*?" Mickey growled, voice gravelly from years of chain-smoking and downing whiskey. He stared into the rear-view mirror at Jimmy for an unsettling amount of time. "Hmmm? The *locals* gonna escort you out there? Huh? They gonna drive you around like Miss Daisy, too?"

Mickey pressed the brakes and slowed the vehicle.

Jimmy's eyes grew wide.

The old man had called his bluff.

As the truck buzzed across the raised shoulder ridges on the asphalt and veered onto the shoulder, Jimmy swallowed hard.

"*Look…*" Jimmy backtracked.

Mickey leaned an elbow on his door and squeezed his wrinkled forehead between his fingers.

Notches rolled his eyes from the passenger seat. The wolfdog's head swung back and forth expectantly, taking turns looking at both of the men from the middle seat.

"I'm building a company that you two can grow with, and I want a spot that's gonna breed success. This lodge'll make us *all* an obscene amount a' green if all goes well. I want both of you *with me* on this. And for that to happen, you boys can't be bickering every *five* seconds." He shook his head with disappointment. "Mickey, how long have I known you?"

There was a long silence, and then, Mickey begrudgingly replied, "You *know* how long."

Mickey opened the door and thrust himself out of the idling truck. Jimmy whipped his door open, too, and followed him onto the dry dirt.

"How *long*, Mickey? When did we meet? I want to hear you *say* it."

Mickey pulled out a rumpled pack of smokes and hollered into the vast plains in front of him. "Since the DUI!"

Notches chuckled loudly, giddy at the painful confession. Mickey could hear the sound of his cackles wafting out the open driver's door. He put a cigarette between his lips and snapped his gaze back to Jimmy. "There! *That* what you wanted? To keep me in my *place*? To *humiliate* me in front 'a *Chuckles* over there?"

"Hey! Watch your *tone* with me! You need *me* a *lot* more than I need *you*." Jimmy narrowed his eyes and lowered his voice. "And you *know* it."

"I can't stand him, Jimmy." Mickey pointed two fingers twisted around the cigarette's filter in Notches's direction.

Jimmy stepped close, speaking even quieter now. "Nobody likes Notches, Mick. He's a human Brillo-pad. But he's *good* at what he *does*. He's been working for me for years. Ever since I quit the practice. And now we're expanding, Mick. We are onto bigger and *better* things. I'm offering you the opportunity to be a part of that."

Mickey exhaled a lungful of smoke, eyes clenched tight. "He gets on my freakin' *nerves*, Jim."

"Focus on the *big picture*, buddy." Jimmy turned to him. "You know, when I met you, you were in trouble. This broken, born-and-bred Wyomingite stumbled into my Denver office. Said he got pulled over on his way to the Denver airport. I worked for you for *months*, Mick. Scouring footage, pouring over deposition testimony. And what happened?"

He sighed. "You got the case thrown out."

"Dang right, I did. Improper search-and-seizure. If you'd have been adjudicated, you'd be a felon. And felons can't *rifle hunt*."

"That firearm rule is idiotic." Mickey hocked a wad of phlegm into a bush with foliage so sparse it resembled a tumbleweed from an old western.

"And what'd you do? As a thank you? You brought me a gift, didn't ya?"

Mickey fought the urge to smile, failing hard, dimples rising in his thin cheeks. "A Browning long-range bolt-action rifle."

"That's right. 7mm Remington Magnum with a carbon fiber stock and camo finish."

"And a Crimson Trace 4-12 scope. Cost me just about every dime I had." He shook his head and took another puff. "Thing's a work of art."

"Don't I *know* it? That *gun*, Mickey, it revived my passion for all this. When I took that thing out in the woods, it was game over. I was hooked again. And back in those days, you didn't care *how* much I was chargin' you by the hour. You were *still* always excited to talk about my mounts and show off your newest kills. And here we are, years later, headin' out on an expedition into the wild together to scout us someplace perfect."

Jimmy turned back to face Notches. The unobscured sun drilled its rays right into his brown irises, making them look like puddles of honey.

"That guy, he's all talk, Mick. He's been a part of this from the beginning. Practically *ran* my Boulder guide business *for* me while I was wrapping things up at the firm. I need you both. And I'm paying you a lot of money to take me out here and show me the lay of the land."

"I'm still not sold on the idea of what we're even *doin'*." Mickey sighed, expelling another lungful of smoke. "I mean, in Colorado, it was...

weekend warriors with bottomless bank accounts payin' to be led right to a kill. It's *unearned. Undeserved.* A *true* hunter put in the *hours,* Jim. They *stalk.* Study the *terrain.*"

"I *get* that. But what would you *rather* have? Enough money to buy your *own* mountain paradise in a couple years or… a huntin' spot? *Think,* Mickey. Use your head. I know you need the money. I know your trailer's fallin' apart. Work with me here, and you'll have a *house.* One that's paid for in no time. All you gotta do is help me lead some idiots with platinum cards around in the woods so they can have a chance at killin' somethin' they can be proud of."

Mickey looked at his remaining cigarette stub for a long moment and then back at Notches, who was still seated in the truck, studying the men. Keeka's tongue hung low, and she panted again, eyes locked on something in the distance.

"Move past whatever beef you have with that numskull, and let's go do this."

Mickey nodded subtly. "*Alright.*"

Just then, a massive herd of antelope bounded through the plains in front of them, bouncing like huge, tan-and-white jackrabbits through the dirt and patches of tall grass. Jimmy watched them, smiling, feeling the metaphorical dollar signs swell in his pupils. "See that?"

"Yeah. *Speed-sheep.* So what?" Mickey shrugged like a sad child.

"It's a *sign,* Mick. We're on the right track." Jimmy nudged him with an elbow. "C'mon. I've been dyin' to see this place ever since you showed me all those blurry pictures in my office." He chuckled.

Mickey flicked his butt near a patch of dry brush below him. He ground it into the powdery earth and nodded.

"If you guys are done *making out* over there, I'd *love* to--"

Jimmy cut Notches off. "We're coming!" He rolled his eyes at Mickey.

Mickey snickered.

Overhead, a bird screeched through the wide-open sky, cruising through the air with graceful ease. Jimmy looked up, shielding his eyes.

"Oh wow, is that a bald eagle?"

Mickey squinted up at it and managed a little smile. "Well, *I'll be.*"

2

It was shortly before the morning's dawn when the creatures of the Great Timbers began their day. Squirrels and raccoons scuttled around, gathering food for breakfast and carrying armfuls of wild berries and nuts back to their young. Herds of deer, antelope, and elk grazed together in the meadow near the edge of the woods on delicious, dewy grass. Foxes darted through the brush with playful abandon, rounding up their omnivorous pups and hunting for earthworms and insects on the forest floor. The lone moose helped shed the woody birch and cherry trees of their leaves, delighting in the delectable browse. Groundhogs, rabbits, and moles scurried into their holes and tunnels, often with fine bounties of scavenged vegetation and earthworms for the winter months ahead.

Even the beaver, Richard, waved a soaking, black hand to greet his community of longtime friends from the thin stream on the edge.

Shedding boughs swayed as a crisp breeze wafted through the land. Fall had arrived, bringing with it a wildly prismatic array of foliage, all in vibrant hues. Soon, winter would screech everything to a frozen halt, transforming the autumnal landscape into a wonderland of snow and ice.

The animals rejoiced in both their privacy and the seemingly endless supply of food and water the Great Timbers provided their loved ones.

Most were friendly and amicable not only to their own species but to others as well. The society had learned to work together, and not just *survive* together, but to *thrive* together. Through time, they'd learned to live in harmony, generously sharing in the bountiful spoils of the forest.

But they still had much to fear.

Namely, famine during the harsher, sparser months, where fruit trees were encrusted with layers of dense snow, and also the presence of the carnivorous predators lurking in the mountains beyond the woods. Creatures that occasionally came down into the forest to feast on cared-for members of the community.

Bears, wolves, and mountain lions lurked up there, among others that had not yet discovered the bevy of options at their disposal. The animals of the Great Timbers took great care to protect each other, always on the lookout for nefarious predators who sought to feed on the meat of the small and peaceful things inhabiting the meadow below.

Several generations prior, the squirrels and raccoons formed a treetop watch in the pines at the base of the mountain, assigning shifts and promptly alerting the critters below whenever they spotted something malicious making its way into the Great Timbers, though they rarely seemed to need it these days.

The mountain creatures still lurked, though, disinclined by the abundant plants on the treacherously steep slopes. Many of the watchers had become lax and careless in their duties at the daily lack of danger, time and time again, using the treetops more as a vantage point to spy on the daily drama on the forest floor below. They stopped believing the seemingly tall tales the older generations would spout, chalking them up to wild yarns or even signs of changing times.

After having gone so long without an incident, there seemed to be little reason for the animals of the Great Timbers to worry.

Life, as they knew it, was good.

3

Ross was one of the most mischievous raccoons in the forest, happy and always trying to cause his own fun brand of trouble for the others. Instead of helping the others collect food, he'd perch on higher boughs and hurl nuts at the squirrels, often making them scatter and flee, dropping their bounty.

On this day, he hid high up in a scrawny birch tree in the middle of a bustling highway of critter activity. He waited patiently for the next unsuspecting creature to walk his way so he could bean them with a walnut. Though tired of his antics, the animals of the forest and meadow knew that Ross never intended to cause any real harm to others. The oft-infuriating raccoon simply derived joy from mischief.

That morning, as usual, the bucks and bulls worked in tandem to teach the young calves and yearlings useful tools and life skills, like how to properly time their foraging, identifying what *not* to eat, how to run faster, and how to use their small spikes for sparring.

Rabbits and groundhogs sat in the entrances of their burrows and tunnels, laughing at the young, clumsy herds flopping about, always a consistent source of amusement.

Down on the floor of the meadow, below the thin limb Ross was seated on, Big Bob attempted to teach his elk son, Ryan, and Ryan's best friend, Edward, a white-tail deer, how to spar with their newly-grown spikes.

All the animals of the Great Timbers respected Big Bob, revering him as their majestic leader of sorts. He was the oldest and largest bull elk around, with a harem of stunning elder sows always nearby. He stood much taller than the other elk, regal and awe-inspiring, with the widest rack of horns.

He was the *strongest* animal in Great Timbers, too. For this reason alone, many of the animals hung on his every word, looking to him for guidance, wisdom, and protection.

Everyone, that is, except the misbehaving Ross. The raccoon did not seem to subscribe to the notion of an elk, or *anyone* for that matter, as a leader.

Overhead, Ross palmed a large walnut, still in its shell, and positioned himself on the branch. He launched it at a calculated moment, factoring in the height of the tree, gravity, the movement of the desired target below, and the wind.

Out of the corner of his eye, Big Bob saw the nut coming and dodged to the side. It smacked his yearling son right on one of his spikes instead.

"*Ow*," Ryan mewed, scrunching his eyes at the harsh vibrations that rattled him.

Big Bob bugled in anger, his bellow escalating to a squelching whistle, followed by a warning grunt, "*Ross!*" He raised his head high in a display of dominance and frustration.

Richard, the beaver, tried to stifle his laughter but nearly fell over when he erupted. This was morning entertainment at its finest in the meadow.

Ryan craned his scrawny neck skyward, "Ross, quit clowning around before my father puts a hoof upside your head!"

"I'd like to see him *try*," Ross called back, tickled by the aggravation on the faces below him. By now, he had a sizeable hazelnut locked-and-loaded.

Big Bob scowled with fierce, black eyes as he charged the tree the raccoon was in. He thrust himself at it so hard that the birch bowed over like a sapling from the power of his nine-hundred-pound body. Roots emerged from the soil with a dull crunch.

The devastating impact sent Ross tumbling down the branches, struggling to dig his claws in enough to stop or slow him so he wouldn't plummet straight to his death, but they couldn't find purchase.

Nearly two-thirds of the way down, his nails finally sunk in, but his weight dragged him down the side until he dropped onto crunchy leaves at the tree's base.

Big Bob bucked his head down at the soil, encasing the masked creature in a pronged prison of impenetrable bone and peeling velvet. "Next time my boy talks, you had *better* listen!" He flashed a thousand-yard stare down at the frightened little mammal.

Ross hyperventilated against the pile of wind-swept leaf litter. "I-I-I was o-only playin'!" He swallowed hard, staring up with fearful, banded eyes while quaking in fear.

"You could *blind* someone that way," the bull barked.

After a long silence, Big Bob showed a graceful mercy, releasing the fur-covered troublemaker from the makeshift holding cell with a frustrated grunt. Ross stood up and brushed dried pine needles and debris from his coat.

Big Bob turned back to concentrate on sharpening the skills of the calves, eyes narrowed with suspicion.

Up in the trees, the squirrels stared at the spectacle. They'd witnessed the whole scene, beady eyes drawn to the exciting drama of their ring-tailed brethren instead of to the mountain's base behind them.

"What're *you* looking at?!" Ross scoffed.

The smattering of gray watchmen burst into a hearty laugh. One of them nearly fell off his branch with his gleeful chuckling.

From the forest floor, Richard, the destructive beaver, found it all *wildly* amusing.

Humiliated by the encounter, Ross kicked a rotten pinecone into the woods and walked off, away from the herd.

As the meadow critters went back to their activities and rituals, the watchmen found themselves distracted by the gossip-like chatter about the hubbub that had just taken place.

So much so that none of them noticed the approaching predator creeping stealthily down the base of the mountain, watching the forest creatures between the gaps of trees, stalking silently…

About to change life as they knew it *forever*.

4

Ross wandered off into the woods, still embarrassed by the encounter with Big Bob, pondering ways to salvage his reputation and save face when he returned. Frustrated, he picked up nuts and pinecones along the way and chucked them at trees, practicing his aim and releasing his angst.

He stopped at the base of a massive jack pine. He dragged his finger pads along the gnarled roots, jutting up from the dry dirt, filled with the urge to climb. He grabbed the trunk and thrust himself up against it, squirming his way up, writhing his belly along the rough bark. From a treacherous height, he scurried out along one of the branches.

From the top of the tree, he could see the entirety of the Great Timbers. Squirrels scurrying and leaping around the forest floor looked like ants from the great height.

In the distance, he heard Ryan and Edward practicing ramming spikes and goading each other with antagonistic comments.

Clackity-Clack!

They awkwardly sparred.

That's gotta hurt, Ross thought as he watched them butt heads. He felt superior up there as if he were lording over the other animals. As if his humiliation had never taken place.

Almost as if he had been triumphant with Big Bob earlier instead of *trembling in fear.*

But his daydream of triumph was fleeting. His smile eroded like the sandy inlet of their stream. His eyes grew wide with shock.

There, on the forest floor, stalking quietly toward the meadow, was the largest grizzly he'd ever seen.

In fact, it was the *only* grizzly he'd ever seen.

I've got to warn the others, he thought.

Ross jumped from branch to branch in a feverish attempt to warn the animals of the bear's presence. He scrambled as fast as his legs would take him, racing down the trunk and over to the trees at the end of *Watchman's Line.*

"Morning, Ross," Heather, a red squirrel, shouted, clutching the trunk of a nearby tree.

But Ross didn't hear the greeting, nor did he have time for conversation.

He *had* to warn Big Bob!

He had to get the bull to bugle an alarm for all to hear!

They'd listen to *him*.

He threw himself at another tree, clawing and writhing his way up the side, panting and huffing, scrabbling with all his might.

He could see the squirrels milling about in the treetops above him, all facing the wrong direction, staring at the youngsters in the meadow.

He screeched, "Guys! Guys!"

"Is that Ross?" Langston, a young gray squirrel, shouted with a giggle.

Just as the gray and red squirrels of *Watchman's Line* turned their attention to Ross, the branch beneath him cracked.

"Oh no."

SNAP!

The whole thing collapsed, taking the raccoon with it. Ross careened to the forest floor, smashing hard into the dirt, the fall rendering him unconscious.

5

The men of *Watchman's Line* looked down at Ross and giggled, some doubling over and clutching their pained little bellies with raucous laughter.

Heather raced over from her tree and rushed to the kit's aid, taking his masked face in her tiny red hands. "Oh no! Ross!"

She caressed the tufts of fur jutting out of his cheeks and stared at his rolled-back eyes with heartfelt concern. "Please, speak to me!"

His body was limp in her grasp, yap slung open wide, pink tongue lolling between narrow sets of snow-white teeth.

"Ross, wake up!"

Slowly, the kit opened his eyes.

"Are you… alright?" Heather held her breath.

Ross was dazed from the fall, trying to focus his juddering eyes on the blurred lines of her lush, taupe eyelashes.

Suddenly, as her beautiful face came into focus, the blood in his veins turned to ice.

The grizzly!

Almost as quickly as he'd hit the ground, Ross remembered the danger he'd been trying to warn the watchmen about. He pulled away from Heather and scrambled towards the meadow as quick as his small legs could carry him.

"Move!" He rushed past a group of milling rabbits chewing foliage, thrashing blades of tall grass aside. "Big Bob! Big Bob, where are you?!"

One of the owls overhead looked down at Ross and twisted its head wildly back and forth at the sight of the poor boy clumsily scrambling.

"Big Bob… there's a… *bear*!" He gasped for air. "Big Bob! Help!"

As he made his way around a throng of trees, he suddenly skidded to a dusty halt.

He was too late.

Ross was terrified.

Across the meadow, the full-grown grizzly stalked its way to the edge of the clearing where the yearlings were fully engrossed in their strenuous daily exercises.

But Big Bob had long-sensed the danger. His eyes were steely and unblinking, trained on the apex predator.

The grizzly stepped out into the open turf of the meadow, revealing itself with a chilling grin on its curling, black lips. It stared at the mighty elk.

The animals were zeroed in on each other, ready for a fight.

One by one, the others throughout the meadow noticed the impending showdown, halting their exercises.

As they understood what was happening, their tiny spikes and horns shot up into the air, all eyes trained on the foreign threat invading their idyllic safe haven. Young deer and elk stood tense, muscles frozen in fear, dark eyes locked on the threat.

"Go!"

Big Bob's bark shook the air around them with his impressively loud command.

All of the young creatures heeded the order, rushing into the timberline.

All that is, except Ryan and Edward, who, small as they were, were still hesitant to leave Big Bob without backup. They knew he would be furious at the refusal, but they stayed locked in place.

"Ryan, Edward, get to safety," Big Bob barked. "*Now!*"

"No, Dad!" Ryan narrowed his eyes at the bear.

But all it took was for Big Bob to whirl his head around and flash that intimidating gaze at the boys. "It wasn't a question. Go!"

He followed with a furious warning bugle, long and clear.

The two yearlings finally followed the order, trudging with reluctance to a spot behind the mighty leader, never peeling their gaze from the grizzly.

Other animals watched intently from behind tree trunks or from the protection of their burrows and branches, each silent and filled with curiosity at how it would all play out.

Ross, on the other hand, bounded on all fours from the timberline toward the bear. The grizzly watched the kit race up a tree, only a few yards away, in admiration of the animal's blended mix of courage and stupidity. But the bear wasn't about to waste effort on a snack, albeit a surely delectable one when much more filling prey was so close.

Ross leaped and scuttled across the overhead boughs until he reached an outstretched limb of a hazelnut tree near the bear. Shaking with fear, he gathered nuts and flashed a scared glance at Big Bob. He didn't know much about bears but hoped with all his might that they were too large and uncoordinated to climb.

"Who's there?" Big Bob's voice boomed through the forest at the massive predator.

The bear rose to her hind feet, bathing a large swath of the meadow floor in darkness.

Most of the animals had never seen an animal larger than Big Bob. He was huge, even for an elk, but the bear was *enormous*. She was hulking, towering like a fur-covered boulder and just as heavy as one.

Big Bob swallowed hard, never having seen such a Goliath up close before.

"*Kilgore*," the bear said as she lowered back down to her front paws with a twisted smile on her face.

Ross could feel the impact shake the tree beneath his soft paws.

"We came from the mountains beyond, my cubs and I. We're here for food. And, well, here you are." Kilgore licked her large, sharp teeth. "It's nothing *personal*, you understand."

Just then, two young cubs emerged from the treeline behind Kilgore, tumbling and rolling like soft balls of fur onto the wavering meadow grass.

Ryan stepped forward to get a better view of the cubs. He'd never seen a bear before. He'd only heard whispered legends and cautionary tales of the near-mythical creature.

The cubs stepped toward Ryan and Edward with inquisitive looks on their round, soil-brown faces.

"Come no closer!" Big Bob was stern and loud. "We want no trouble from you! Or *them*. I demand you move on!"

"You *demand*?" Kilgore chuckled, waltzing casually toward the bull.

The two cubs, following their mother's lead, crept closer to Ryan and Edward, each one eyeing a different animal.

But when they opened their mouths to speak, they were disarming.

"My name's Arnold. This is my brother, Wesley."

The cubs smiled genuinely, unaware that they were supposed to present as any sort of a threat.

From the tone of his voice, Ryan could tell they were less malicious than he'd initially thought. The young elk stretched his neck to look taller. "I'm Ryan. This is my best friend, Edward."

"What is this," roared Kilgore at her cubs, "some kind of *social* meeting? Boys, they are not your friends. They're *dinner*."

Arnold and Harold backed away from Ryan and Edward. Kilgore turned to the tree behind her and swung at it with her massive paws, tearing bark off with thick, unforgiving nails.

Arnold and Harold were petrified. They'd never seen their mother this infuriated before.

High above them, a far climb above, Ross was in the tree, hazelnut ammo in his smooth palms.

Waiting.

"Ryan? Edward? Go into the woods. Do you hear me?" Big Bob growled without taking his eyes off Kilgore.

A silence befell the meadow.

"I won't tell you again," he bellowed. "Go!"

The yearlings galloped away from the bear, straight into the line of jackpines and birch. Once at a safer distance, Ryan turned around.

"Come on, Ryan. You heard him," Edward said, clearly shaken.

But Ryan didn't budge. He fought the urge to trot cautiously back toward his father, freezing in place instead.

Kilgore roared out with fury, her voice booming across the meadow.

A flock of sparrows took off from the boughs of a nearby birch and fluttered away, making their skyward trek far beyond the mountain.

Kilgore stomped her wide paws onto the dry grass with vibrating thumps and took off toward the bull elk.

Big Bob flexed his sturdy legs and lowered his horns, staring at her through their pointed, bony protrusions, prepared to charge.

The huge bear took off across the meadow, grunting all the way, seeking to sink her sharp teeth into Big Bob's tender flesh.

When she was halfway there, Big Bob charged her, launching himself with all of the speed that he possessed. He *had* to defend the meadow filled with beings he'd been sworn to protect.

With antlers down and powerful legs thrusting into the squishy soil below his hooves, the mighty elk slammed, hard and fast, horns-first into Kilgore, stopping the massive beast in her tracks with his piercing rack.

Kilgore roared in pain, scrambled backward, and stood up. She looked at the tears in the flesh of her chest. Instead of retreating, she flashed an evil smile and, without further warning, charged at the bull elk again.

The grizzly was *determined* to feast.

She grabbed Big Bob by the antlers and wrenched him viciously down onto his side with her powerful limbs.

Kilgore sensed the power of her formidable foe as the elk squirmed to twist free of the bear's grasp.

She bared her sharp teeth. Saliva flowed from the corners of her mouth as she stared at Big Bob's exposed neck.

He struggled to break free.

The animals of the Great Timbers watched the gruesome spectacle, helpless to do anything about it. Some huddled in fear, ready to flee if the grizzly turned her deadly attention to them.

One good slash into that maned throat and dinner is served, Kilgore thought.

Ross, who was watching from the tree just above the cubs, grabbed the largest nut in his arsenal and took aim at Kilgore.

The bear tightened her grip on Big Bob's horns, clacking her maw open and shut, biting at his neck, struggling to sink into any meat through all of the thrashing. As soon as her teeth could take hold, the elk would thrash her about again, and she'd lose her grip.

Big Bob twisted and turned to thwart the bear's attack, but the 800-pound predator was unbelievably strong, weighing just under what he, himself, did.

Kilgore roared into the air, fiendish teeth glistening with pink drool.

She dove her mouth down toward the elk's throat again…

CRACK!

Something smashed her right in the head.

CRACK, CRACK!

The impact agitated her. She looked up in the trees to locate the source of the annoyance. Kilgore saw the raccoon standing there, little arm cocked, ready to throw again.

She roared at Ross, loud and powerful.

You could blind someone that way! Big Bob's words replayed in his mind.

Ross fired his next hazelnut, throwing it with all the strength he could muster, ignoring the bear's roaring jaw completely.

BAM!

The hurled nut struck Kilgore in the left eye.

Bingo.

Ross smiled to himself.

She was stunned that such a small creature would be idiotic enough to take on a beast of her size.

Pain followed. Her eye throbbed, and every time she opened it, it watered.

Kilgore opened her mouth and let out an earth-shattering roar, covering her eye with her massive paw.

This was the opportunity that Big Bob needed.

As Ross chucked the next nut, the elk thrust his large rack forward, smashing the moaning grizzly under the chin. The force from Big Bob's blow knocked the beastly behemoth backward, as well as himself.

Kilgore rounded her spine and clutched her injured face.

Before the bear could blink her one uninjured eye, Big Bob was back on all four hooves, horns lowered, charging again with all of the strength he had left.

The exhausted elk's horns rammed into the predator, once again cutting through the tough, hairy hide of Kilgore's chest.

Kilgore roared, nearly deafening Big Bob.

Blood dribbled from the wounds in her chest where the horns pierced.

How could this be, she wondered. *Bested by an elk?*

She was embarrassed to be in such a state of defeat by her dinner in front of the cubs. Both of her children, by now, were alarmed and concerned for their mother's waning safety.

Big Bob stepped backward and prepared to charge again.

Kilgore was hurt, and she knew it.

If she wanted redemption and to save face in front of her boys, she was going to have to finish what she started.

She shook off the pain, then glared back at Big Bob, who was poised, positioned for another brutal attack.

"I'm impressed," snarled Kilgore, groaning as she readied herself for defense, blinking tears from her blurred left eye.

BAM!

A walnut smacked her in the back of the head. She didn't turn around. Instead, she locked eyes with Big Bob.

"I ought to send my boys up that tree to feast on your little masked pal. We'll be too busy, though, feasting on your backstraps while the little nut-chucker watches."

Without another word, Kilgore charged Big Bob, pounding the ground with percussive thumps as she raced full-force at the massive elk.

Big Bob sprang forward on his hind legs. Both animals came together, colliding on the ground with a violent force that seemed to rock the Great Timbers.

Kilgore bucked her head upwards and deflected Big Bob's antlers with a blow that nearly broke the bull's neck. She swung a huge paw at the elk's shoulder, and her long, sharp claws tore into him.

A shock wave of pain rippled through the majestic mammal. Big Bob's pained screams and bleats echoed through the meadow.

Blood trickled slowly from the claw marks that had ripped through his torso.

But there was no time to stop and assess the damage. Kilgore was fastidiously determined to kill Big Bob.

Kilgore attacked again, snarling her snout, uttering another fearsome, low growl into the air.

She grabbed hard and wrenched his horns, flipping the wounded elk onto his back. His shoulder was shredded and bleeding. He was growing weak from the fight and his injury, too weak to attack again.

"Dad," Ryan barked out from nearby. His terrified voice drew the attention of his father's vicious attacker.

Kilgore smiled at the cluster of yearlings watching helplessly from the side of the meadow, knowing they, too, would be easy prey once the bull was finally incapacitated.

With Big Bob's throat in her sights, Kilgore knew victory was hers.

Just as the bear lowered her head toward Big Bob's exposed throat, something stopped her.

Something was *wrong*.

Something was *very* wrong…

Kilgore sniffed the elk, then raised her head to the sky and inhaled deeply.

What was that smell?

Kilgore had smelled it before. Somewhere…

Nearly a lifetime ago.

But what was it?

It smelled like… *a threat.*

The bear sniffed again, keenly attuned to the faint waft of something foreign in the air, then released her hold on Big Bob and backed away.

The badly wounded elk tumbled to the ground, confused.

"Arnold! Wesley! Come now," Kilgore roared. The cubs obeyed without hesitation, and the sleuth of bears ambled quickly away from the meadow, toward the base of the mountain range, noses in the air.

From the floor of the meadow, Big Bob lay injured on his side, watching the baffling and sudden retreat, wondering what had made Kilgore turn tail and run.

After the bears were gone, Ryan bounded to his father as fast as his knobby legs would go. He looked down at Big Bob's bleeding shoulder, then softly nuzzled up to the elk.

"Dad! I thought I was going to lose you!"

The bull smiled at the yearling's affection with all of the love a father could have for a son.

He winced and bugled in pain as he made his way onto his feet. It strained him to stand. Blood drizzled down his thick mane in matted rivulets, but his muscles ached more than anything.

Fighting off the bear had taken every bit of strength within him.

Big Bob angled his bleeding neck at an odd angle to look up at the tree above him where Ross was perched.

"Thank you," the elk uttered, pain in his voice.

"I had to do *something*," Ross replied.

"You were brave in the face of danger. Thank you."

The irony was not lost upon him. No, he realized how he'd chastised the raccoon for the very same action hours before, which he was genuinely and thoroughly appreciative of now.

Ross was overwhelmed by the simple utterance. No one had ever taken the kit's trained arm and throwing skills seriously before, and yet, here was the greatest leader of his time, making him feel like a hero in front of the others. Ross smiled, joy spreading through his furry little body.

Across the meadow, the other animals, sensing the danger had passed with the retreat of the grizzlies, emerged.

Big Bob and Ryan shuffled slowly across the tall grass plain toward the line of gleeful, cheering animals, all relieved to see their leader up and walking so soon after the attack.

Ross climbed down out of the tree and joined them for a somber yet victorious march.

Big Bob slowly limped on, looking down at the raccoon. "Ross, tonight you'll be revered as the soldier you are."

* * *

Beyond the meadow, on a ridge overlooking the grassy terrain surrounded by the Great Timbers, a hunter pulled his dull, blue eyes away from his spotting scope. He smiled, flashing a mouthful of abused, nicotine-stained teeth, giddy at the find. He folded up the tripod, packed the scope in its case, and gathered the rest of his gear for the trek back to camp.

Mickey was a withered, scrawny man who'd spent most of his adult life in pursuit of trophy-kills and mounts that would make other hunters green with envy.

Today, he saw two contenders, ones that made the years-long search finally worthwhile.

He pulled a tiny pad of paper and a short pen from his woodland camouflage jacket pocket and sketched a rough map of the ridge, mountains, meadow, and dense woods beyond. It was a crude map, but it would do the trick.

He tucked it away in the breast pocket of his flannel long-sleeve shirt and pulled a fresh cigarette out of the pack stored in the same compartment. He shoved it between his chapped, grinning lips and lit it with the lighter in his pocket.

What a fight, he thought to himself. *Thank God they didn't kill each other.*

No, he giggled to himself.

That's my job.

He sneered for a moment, squinting from the blinding brightness of the fiery orb in the sky, one that sat amid the colorful sunset. He scanned the lush foliage below, the greenery surrounding the meadow that had to be a mile away or more as the crow flies.

As his eyes stayed trained on the meadow, thoughts of a taxidermied grizzly in mid-roar or the elk's mounted head adorning his trophy room roiled in his brain.

He wasn't sure which one he wanted more.

Both, if he was being honest.

Finally, he broke from his trance and stepped cautiously off the rocky platform and made his way back down the ridge toward camp, disappearing into the shadowy thicket.

7

As night fell upon the inhabitants of the Great Timbers, the squirrels and rabbits worked tirelessly to build a bed of leaves for Big Bob to rest on. With a strained look of appreciation, he carefully bedded down.

The active bleeding had stopped, but the muscles in his neck and haunches ached from the battle. His open wound felt deep.

Some rodents gathered medicinal plants that would surely help their injured leader. They offered the healing herbs, and he munched on the vegetation with a soft mew of gratitude.

Heather even went back and forth into the woods to bring him fresh forbs, tree bark, and chewed-off branches from some of the elk's favorite shrubs.

Some of the ladies of the harem made a poultice. Richard carefully applied it to his injuries with his freshly stream-washed little hands. They hoped the remedies would ease the elk's pain and stave off infection.

Edward and Ryan bedded down by Big Bob.

"Are you… going to be *okay*, Dad," Ryan asked.

"Everything'll be alright," Big Bob assured him weakly. He rubbed his nose against his son's spotted coat and winced, almost imperceptibly, at the pain it caused to do so.

"He's strong, Ryan," Edward piped up, eyes full of adoration for their majestic protector.

"You're right." Ryan smiled slightly. "Soon, he'll be healed enough to teach us how to fight a bear, just like *he* did."

That warmed Big Bob's heart.

Though it hurt him to do so, he spoke. "Help me stand, boys, if you will."

"Of course, Dad." Ryan's voice was soft, eyes wide. He nudged his head under the crook of his father's neck and lifted. Ryan joined him in the struggle to get the elk on his feet again.

Big Bob mustered the strength to walk slowly to the moonlit stream, where he lowered his head to the running water to drink. Every swallow jabbed sharply through his injured muscles.

Big Bob looked back at where he and Kilgore had tangled hours before. The tall grass was still disheveled there.

He spoke softly, "Boys, come with me. It's time you knew that there are worse threats to the creatures of the Great Timbers than a family of hungry grizzlies."

* * *

Deep in the woods, the three trekked at Big Bob's honey-drip of a pace to an area divided by a sloping rock wall where the children weren't permitted.

Even the adults were discouraged from grazing or foraging there.

"The elders said we aren't allowed here, sir," Edward said timidly.

"You aren't. And I'm about to show you why. After what happened today, it is important that you know something. Now, be careful around that pit. If you fall in there, you perish. We lost my great, great uncle in that one."

The bull motioned with his head to a massive pit dug into the ground. As the boys passed it, Ryan could see sharpened spikes protruding from the dark floor of it, their pointy edges barely visible in the moonlight.

As the three trekked up the winding slope to the top of a low, bush-shrouded butte, Big Bob stayed quiet and solemn.

As they turned the corner into the clearing at the top, they saw a large cache of metal devices, string, rope, and flattened animal pelts all piled together in the center like some sort of morbid treasure trove.

"Woah! What is all this?!" Ryan's eyes were alight with wonder as he galloped awkwardly over to the mound of supplies.

"Careful, son." Big Bob was stern, pinching his eyes tight from the pain. His tense shoulder muscles, slick with poultice, glistened in the starlight.

Edward sniffed one of the sprung bear traps, awash with a sort of terrified curiosity. His legs trembled. He felt skittish, ready to bolt at the first foreign sound.

But the only sound to come was Big Bob's voice.

"I know you're both only a few years old, but one day, if you're fortunate, you will have your own harem and calves of your own. What I'm about to tell you... it's important that you tell them, too. When I was right about your age, my father was the one teaching the herd how to protect themselves from predators like Kilgore. But bears and mountain lions aren't the only dangers we've faced. There were others then, more ruthless and unfeeling than any grizzly. They stood only on their hind legs. They didn't have antlers or claws. Instead, they used what you see here to claim their prey.

"He brought us here one day. He showed Melvin and me this collection of strange things that have been found in these woods throughout every generation. He called this *the forbidden forest.* It's a place where we bring our most dangerous discoveries, things left by the two-legged creatures. This place is a somber gallery of all of the pain that has come before us and serves as a reminder that there is more to come.

Ryan looked up at his father. "I'm afraid I don't understand."

Edward looked up, too, hanging on the bull's words.

"After that grizzly attacked me today, it was a reminder that I have more that I need to pass on to you boys before I leave this world. There is more than you need to be wary of than just bears and mountain lions. Those hind-legged creatures were ruthless and cold.

Big Bob paused for a moment, swallowing the painful lump in his throat at the images that flashed in his mind. Though long ago, the pain felt fresh.

Edward sniffed a long circular tube of metal and raised his snout to the curved, wooden bit at the end, smelling faint traces of powdery residue. Despite being ravaged by the elements, the scent was there, wafting its peculiar notes into the air around it with the gentle night's breeze.

Big Bob mewed quietly, with great sadness in his tone.

"Ryan, one day, your grandfather was standing in the meadow, the one we stood in today. I was sparring with your uncle. We were battling for your mother." A faint smile crept up onto his face at the thought of her. Then his expression soured again.

"Dad was watching over the herd while they grazed. Suddenly, a loud sound rang across the Great Timbers, a noise none of us had ever heard.

"When we looked toward the sound, my horns still intertwined with your uncles, I saw my father take off toward us, no doubt to corral us all back into the woods. But something was… *wrong* with him. He stumbled, tumbling to the ground in front of me. He was bleeding. *Gasping.*

"As he was laying there, struggling for air, three strange two-legged animals came down from that flat-top ledge up on the mountain and approached him. I wanted to run away, just as he'd taught us, but I didn't want to leave him behind.

"These… creatures had these long stick-like things in their paws." He motioned with his head to the item Edward was sniffing. "That one, to be precise. We all called them *boom-sticks* from that day on because of the sound they made. One of the creatures pointed his at your uncle, Melvin, and the noise from it shook the ground beneath my feet. It was the same sound as before, only much louder."

His face grew even more gravely serious, a look that Ryan wasn't prepared for. "I ran. *We* ran."

With a lump in his throat, the great elk's eyes grew glassy with tears. "The next thing I knew, more elk in our herd had fallen, including your uncle and one of the elder sows."

Big Bob sniffed, nose wet and eyes glimmering like stars in the moonlight. "Melvin dropped, too, just like Dad. Even though I felt like a coward, I ran. I couldn't understand what was happening. I didn't want to end up the same way. I regret leaving them. If there was something I could have done to *help*…"

He sniffed again.

"They made noises, those creatures, different than any animal I'd ever heard, whooping louder than any crane. Then, they did something so *awful* to dad…. and to your *uncle*. Something I've never imagined one animal could do to another."

Ryan and Edward listened closely to the tale. Their small, round eyes were filled with fear.

"Kilgore is a predator; this is true," Big Bob continued. "Bears are vicious, as you now know. But the difference between that bear and those three… monsters is that at least if Kilgore had won, she would have at least *eaten* what she killed. She would have fed her hungry cubs. Though we must protect ourselves from them, we cannot fault others for the lengths they will go to when they are starving. But these two-legged creatures… these *monsters*… didn't want to *eat*. They desecrated our loved ones for *parts*, parts that surely wouldn't feed their hungry bellies. They left the rest to decay as hideous, wasteful, fly-ridden reminders until there was nothing left of our fallen herd members but a meadow of bones. My father was reduced to carrion for the scavengers. These creatures… they simply took the heads and antlers.

They didn't care what they did to our tribe. They didn't care about the families they destroyed."

He felt as if a surge of icy water washed through him. It sent a subtle shiver through his muscular legs.

"As fast as they'd come, they were gone, too. Those animals with their *boom-sticks* disappeared into the woods with their wasteful prizes. I've waited for their return for years, but so far, they've never shown their faces since. Much of this was here when I was a calf. We have only added to it, stockpiling anything that we find that seems to pose a danger to our people. This pile is an important reminder that they will return, whatever they are."

He gritted his omnivorous molars to keep from crying. "I hope on those stars above that it will not be during our lifetime."

Big Bob stifled the well of emotion rising within him. "You must learn to run quick as lighting and always be ready for anything, boys. Be clever. Be smart. And stay fast, always. Speed and sparring skills will help you protect the herd when I'm no longer around. Understand?"

"Yes, sir!" The fearful yearlings responded in unison.

8

Mickey had walked east for a little over a mile as night fell like a thick blanket atop him. He'd been carefully watching the ground through his arduous trek, careful not to step on any slumbering rattlesnakes or break an ankle in a gopher hole.

When he finally looked up, a smile spread across his withered face. He saw the lights of the camp just off in the distance. His pace quickened. The sweet rush of relief coursed through his veins. He reached into his pocket to feel for the map he'd made of the spot where his greatest trophy was soon to be claimed.

He slid his fingers behind the paper, plucked out a cigarette, and popped it between his thin, chapped lips. Shuffling briskly, he cupped his hands, flicked open his lighter, and lit it.

Thinking of his future conquest, he smiled and sucked in a deep lungful of smoke. He had to be careful of what he told the others about what he had seen.

He didn't want to take any chances.

Those trophies were to be claimed by him and him alone.

Even though he hadn't drawn bear or elk tags himself this year, he was determined to finally bring home a long-coveted trophy for his foyer.

To Mickey, his taxidermist was a true *artist*. One with pieces more exciting than any Monet or Van Gogh. Months after discovering his taxidermist's shop, he found his own home adorned with various kills, each poised in eerie states of seized life. After all, he believed that animals were put on this earth for man. For mastication. For recreation. And, heck, even for *decoration*.

Despite being outside the season for elk or bear, big trophy mount opportunities were rare.

Tomorrow, he'd live out his dream.

Regardless of the law.

All creatures, large and small, were fair game… Even if they weren't in season.

Hunting was year-round to Mickey.

In fact, though he'd never tell a soul, many of the mounts adorning the flat surfaces of his home were poached illegally, without a tag.

Tomorrow's kill would be no different.

The woods were vast, wardens were few, and Mickey, a man of Irish descent who believed the stereotypes, had always prided himself on being somewhat *lucky*.

As he approached camp, the men inside the tent suddenly roared with a loud burst of wild laughter. He sighed, thinking of how many creatures would be put off by the noise the men were emitting. Sound carried far beyond the camp. The animals were sensitive to it.

…Not to mention the *Department of Game and Fish*. The last thing Mickey needed was further attention drawn to the area while Jimmy was funding this trip. They didn't need some hyper-vigilant goody-two-shoes game warden sticking his public-servant nose in their business.

The shelter was a military-grade triage tent purchased from an Army-Navy Surplus store that had gone belly-up in Aurora a few years back. The structure was large enough to house ten, so it fit the three men just fine with plenty of room to spare. It reminded Mickey of a beige circus tent and ol' Jimmy the *carnival barker*.

Leading up to this expedition, Jimmy had sprung for some fold-out military-style cots, a deluxe kerosene camp stove, a rickety folding table with a set of chairs, a whisper-quiet putt-putt generator, a sturdy game-dressing table, plus a 5-gallon plastic camp toilet as an added convenience on the colder nights.

Mickey opened the flap, dropped his smoke on the ground, and crushed the smoldering butt with the sole of his boot before strolling inside.

"Well, look who finally made it back," Jimmy chuckled. "Thought you got lost, Mick. We were about to go pokin' around for you in the coyote scat."

Mickey faked a smile. "Gonna take more than a dog to take *me* down."

He plopped his weary body down with an audible groan on his stiff cot and tossed his spotting scope kit on the ground beside his rifle case. He twisted, cracking the vertebrae in his lower back like a glow stick, and then joined the other men at the table in the warm glow of the kerosene-fueled camp stove.

"How'd the scout go? See anything of interest?" Jimmy looked up from the playing cards in his hand, brown eyes glinting in the nearby flame.

Mickey lied and shook his head, careful not to let his eyes light up at the memory of the grizzly and elk he'd watched in the meadow.

"Dang." Jimmy tossed his cards on the table and chewed his bottom lip, deep in thought.

A former Denver defense lawyer, Jimmy had given up his career and pivoted to his passion, rising in the ranks until he was one of the wealthiest outfitters in the Midwest. If you wanted to go deer hunting in Colorado, all you had to do was send him an email. Before you knew it, you were on the trail to big game with his skilled guide, Notches, to lead you to the kill.

It was all perfectly legal back in the beginning.

It had to be, with *his* reputation.

He, at times, even considered it a public service. He was helping rifle and bow hunters fulfill their wildest dreams. For the right price, *every* hunter could return home with bragging rights, satisfied with their bounty.

However, with the increase in the state's tag allowance in the years since, the animal population in the Colorado Rockies declined. Especially *big game*. The presence of so many hunters had driven them deeper into the woods despite the many well-placed feeders, blinds, and careful attempts to mask their scent.

Every outfitter in the area scrambled to find the next true hunter's paradise. He had the itch to expand, to broaden his horizons to the nearly uninhabited state to the north:

Wyoming.

With only 5 people per square mile, the boxy state was an outdoorsman's *playground*, a massive expanse that man could lose himself in. Ironically, in both the best and *worst* ways possible.

He soon found that eager customers there were, in fact, willing to pay the astronomical fees.

"Saw a small herd of whitetail, decent-sized does," Mickey said, looking at the dirt floor, his voice breaking Jimmy out of his nostalgic trance.

"Deer… deer's good." Jimmy stared down at the arrangement of playing cards in the solitaire formation before him. "No elk, or moose, or nothin'?"

The mention of the word elk made Mickey clam up. He shook his head solemnly.

Notches growled something unintelligible beneath his rank breath while cleaning his rifle. He took pride in his weapon, always maintaining it. He was overly fond of this one in particular, as it was responsible for taking down his greatest conquests. Every time a trophy-sized animal was killed by it, he carved a small notch right on the spine of the stock.

He had twelve notches already and anxiously awaited number thirteen.

After once asking about the tick-marks and hearing the explanation, Jimmy nicknamed him *Notches* from that day forward, rarely ever using his real name, Nicholas, from that point forward.

That day was one Jimmy would always remember. He'd seen the man kill two giant, sparring bucks with one round.

Notches spit a wad of tobacco juice onto the dirt floor, slammed the bolt of the rifle closed, and laid the gun on the table with the barrel facing Mickey.

With two fingers, Mickey reached over to shove it away from him.

Notches glowered at him, sending a chill right through Mickey.

"Did I say you could touch 'at?"

Mickey didn't respond. He just stared at Notches, eyes focused hard on the man's wicked gaze.

"What's the matter?" Notches grinned. "Guns make you nervous?"

"Nope." Mickey kept his eyes locked. "*Idiots* make me nervous."

"Don't start, you guys. I beg of you." Jimmy rolled his eyes and rubbed the bridge of his nose hard. The tension between them grated on his nerves.

Mickey snickered, trying to change the subject. He pointed to the front door of the tent and let his slim hand slap back down onto his thigh with a *smack*. "Dang near got lost on my way back."

Notches shifted his whole body to Mickey, leaning forward with aggression. "How're *you* gettin' *lost* out here? Don't you claim to hunt this land every *year*?"

Mickey looked at Notches out of the corner of his eye. "First off, I said I *nearly* got lost. Secondly, this is a *massive* sprawl of forested land. I'm *human*. Memories fail. Who knows, maybe your mind's like a steel trap." There was venom in his voice. "But I'm guessin' that ain't the case since you gotta carve a notch on 'at thing every time you kill somethin'. What's a-matter, *Nicholas*? Countin' past ten too *hard* for ya'?"

Notches grabbed the rifle off the table and glanced at the stock where he carved his kills. He softly moved his hands over the grooves, then situated it between his arms and pointed the barrel directly at Mickey, poised to take a lethal shot.

"There's room for *another*."

"*Children, children.*" Jimmy swung his arms wide in an effort to calm them both. Though he prided himself on his patience, both as a hunter and as a lawyer, their immature bickering over the last few days had started to wear on him. "Mickey, go calm down. Have a smoke or somethin'."

"Why're you always taking up for him? Why's it always my fault?" Mickey grumbled.

"It's not. Frankly, you're both being cranky, old codgers right now. I need you both to just relax tonight. Tomorrow, we're gonna take the side-by-side over to the lake and take a look at the acreage that I'm probably gonna put the bid in on. You guys are gonna need to start getting along. You are gonna be working together year-round. If you can't play nice, one of you is gonna get the ax. Simple as 'at."

Though he was barely five feet tall, Mickey was tough as nails and scrappy as the day was long. He stared at Notches for a moment and then rose to his feet, shook his head, and stormed out of the tent. Maybe Jimmy was right.

Maybe another cigarette *would* calm his nerves. He wasn't about to let Notches steal his payday.

Once outside, Mickey took a seat on a stump near the ashen remnants of an old campfire.

Keeka trotted over to him, panting excitedly.

Mickey stuffed a bent cigarette between his lips and reached over. He brushed the dog's thick mane of hair and knotted bandanna with his age-spotted hand.

"Can't say I blame you for hangin' outside. I don't want to be around him either."

Her bright eyes glimmered. She listened intently, hanging on his every word.

Mickey caught a glimpse of a small jug of kerosene a few feet behind her, used to refill the space heaters and cooktop. It sat next to a rolling ice chest full of Jimmy's assortment of domestic IPAs near the entrance of the tent.

Suddenly, a *dark* thought occurred to him. Something black from the abyssal corners of his angered mind.

A thought that troubled him deeply, even knowing he was capable of it.

He knew a way to hit Notches where it hurt. A way to finally teach that instigating coot a lesson...

He stared at the dog, wondering if he'd be capable of something so deplorable.

She was a *pet*, after all.

His *pride and joy...*

After a few more long drags, he sunk deeper into the notion that he'd stumbled upon, a suitable form of retribution for the constant jabs and threats.

I'll teach you to point a gun at me, he thought, growing fury clouding his judgment.

Mickey flicked the butt onto the arid soil and ground it in with his hiking boot, leaving the flattened cotton filter there, like one of Hansel & Gretel's breadcrumbs. He stared long and hard for a moment at the jug before his dim, blue eyes flit over to the dog again. She looked up at him and closed her mouth, intently fixed on his face with her belly in the dirt.

He rose with purpose.

Notches decided her fate when he pointed the rifle at my chest.

He strolled over to the cooler. She followed him, trailing the determined man like a downy shadow. He listened to the men murmuring inside the tent. He heard Notches mention his name in a grumble, unsure of what was said but certain it wasn't anything positive from his tone.

Mickey leaned down to pick up the jug and pet Keeka's soft ears. He smiled down at her, excited that she was still by his side.

She leaned into his hand, enjoying the affection, a *rarity* for a hunting dog with an owner like Notches.

Mickey gripped the bandanna in his fist and slid it up over her head. As it grazed her snout, she looked up at him with curiosity.

He unscrewed the bottle cap and doused the red swath of fabric, chilled by the liquid as it dripped down the back of his hand. He returned the jug to the dirt and walked into the woods, past the tent, several feet into the treeline.

Keeka followed.

Mickey knelt down, feeling his bones crackle with the movement. He wasn't as spry as he used to be. He slid his noxious-smelling hand around Keeka's neck and cinched his grip tight and fast, scaring her. She tugged backward, trying to put some distance between them, unsure if he was playing rough or meant her harm.

He held fast. She struggled, hissing with panic, bucking him, and squirming with all her might. The foul scent on his hands alarmed her, filling her ultra-keen senses with a literal air of danger.

Keeka growled.

Mickey brought the cloth up to her face and clamped her jaws with the red rag.

The smell of the kerosene was strong.

She writhed, hissing with fear.

But no one could hear her muffled whines from where they were.

Mickey gritted his teeth and imagined Notches's smug face in the trunk of the jack pine next to him.

Rage pounded in his head.

Keeka fought harder, clawing at her attacker, trying to suck in enough air to growl or bark.

Or to simply *breathe*.

But he had her snout clamped tight with both hands.

She felt dizzy.

Frantic.

Terrified.

Her lungs were on fire, unable to see anything but red rag.

Finally, she used her brawny weight to throw the slim man off-balance. Mickey lost his footing, and he tumbled forward over an exposed tree root, landing hard on his frail knees. His body slammed into the rocky soil, and he stifled a yelp while Keeka struggled free from the rag.

But the old man wasn't stopping without a fight. His hand grasped onto her tracking collar and twisted, turning it into a tightened noose around her neck. She panted and thrashed, once again struggling for air.

Still on his knees, Mickey held tight. The plastic collar snapped in his hands, and he lunged forward, wrapping the crook of his other arm around her neck. He squeezed tightly as if he were trying to choke another human. With his other hand, he reached into the pine needles, snatched the rag back up, and held the fuel-soaked cloth over her snout again.

As the stench filled her lungs, she pounced on him with both front paws and protracted her claws, swiping at him as if he were made of dirt, clawing as if she could dig right through the old man.

"Gah!" He growled, trying hard not to alert the others, heart thudding wild in his bony chest.

He hadn't thought any of this through.

He'd only acted in rage.

He hadn't played out the consequences.

If he got *caught*…

Jimmy and Notches were armed to the hilt.

Notches had a fierce temper, too. He'd shoot first and ask questions later.

And out here in the wilderness, a man's corpse could be lost forever…

What have I done? The thought echoed around and around as Keeka fought for her life in his arms.

She clawed harder, shredding his shirt and spilling the contents of his front pocket on the forest floor. His cigarettes, hand-drawn map, and lighter became buried between layers of pine needles in the tousle. Mickey didn't notice. His mind was a million miles away.

In the dark of the night, Keeka lost consciousness from the fumes. Her body gave in and relaxed into a limp pile of tri-toned hair in the crook of the old man's arm. Her once-brilliant eyes rolled back into her lids, and her struggle finally ceased.

After her body went limp, Mickey removed the cloth and lowered her to the ground. He pulled the bandanna back over her head, resting it around her throat once again.

He stood up, staring at the stilled animal, sweat beading on the concerned wrinkles spread across his forehead.

What would the others would do if they found her like that? Dead, yet unmarred by an attack from something wild? They'd never believe it was that innocent.

Mickey grabbed the wolf-dog by her front legs and tugged her to a thick bush nearby, tucking her beneath the foliage near the base of it, kicking her hard in the ribs repeatedly to hide her fully.

He tossed the broken tracking collar over the steep cliff into the tree-laden depths beyond.

Mickey scooped up an armful of pine needles and shook them all over to cover the drag marks in the layer of amber leaf litter.

He stared, satisfied, at the bush.

Suddenly, his thoughts turned to Notches. To the *degradation* the dog's owner caused inside the tent. A smile crept onto the corner of his mouth as he thought about how much time Notches would hopefully waste the next day looking for her down in the holler.

He imagined the heartbroken look Notches would have plastered on his ugly face if he found her curled up dead under her bushy grave marker.

Without another thought, he strolled back to the tent and ducked through the narrow opening, trying hard to mask his grin as Notches glared at him from over the barrel of a silver revolver he was now in the middle of cleaning.

"You seen Keeka out there," Notches asked as Mickey brushed past.

"Nah." Mickey rinsed his kerosene-soaked hands with the half-filled bottle of water beside his cot, letting the liquid spatter on the dirt below. "Shoot, maybe *she* couldn't stand you either an' took off."

He dried his palms on his pants, changed out of his torn, plaid shirt into some waffled long johns, and crawled under his covers.

Notches set down the pistol and lumbered to the door of the tent, smacking it open, enraged. "Keeka, come 'ere, girl!"

No response.

"Keeka, come on, girl, where are you?"

Still, *nothing.*

Silence.

Notches scanned the darkness beyond their camp but heard nothing beyond an owl screeching in the distance and the chirp of crickets.

Mickey closed his eyes and imagined Notches standing over the dead dog in broad daylight, frozen in a silent scream. He fought the urge to smile and tucked his face beneath the covers.

9

Just beyond the treeline, beneath the thick juniper, Keeka's eyes peeled open. Pain coursed through her bruised ribcage with every inhalation, lungs burning like fire. Sharp pain stung her snout with every labored breath. The overpowering smell of kerosene made her eyes water.

It was in the fur of her face...

On the bandanna wrapped around her bruised throat...

The world was foreign to her. It was *terrifying* through her bleary eyes and drowsy mind.

She had no idea she was only a few short feet away from where she was attacked. She had no clue that a few feet further still, she'd find the back of the tent her master was in.

As she lay there, too weak to move, too weak to even lift her own head, hatred and fear bubbled up in her, sending panic through her pained form.

Replaying Mickey's attack, she felt foolish for ever having shown him kindness. She vowed that *if she lived*, she'd make him pay. In agony, her eyes closed, and she drifted into the darkness once again.

10

About thirty yards from the meadow where Big Bob and the yearlings had gone to bed, and in true, nocturnal fashion, the night's festivities were just getting started for Ross.

In the hours since the attack, Ross had quickly become somewhat of a hero to the treetop community. Having heard the news of his bravery, the squirrels, chipmunks, opossums, and other raccoons from all around the forest came to offer their gratitude to the kit. They brought with them a bounty of nuts and foraged fruits, bestowing them upon the mammal courageous enough to stand up to the ferocious grizzly.

"Ross," Heather cooed with a smile as the raccoon sat down on the ceremonial bed of wood chips appreciative rodents had made for him. "What you did today was so brave." She scurried over, arms filled to the brim with an assortment of boulder raspberries, red elderberries, and currants, laying them all at his feet.

Ross flashed a bashful smile, unsure how to respond. Normally, he erred a little on the arrogant side, but there was something about the beautiful red squirrel that always took him off-guard and made him blush.

Fortunately, before he could stumble on his words, a gathering of the young watchmen trainees interrupted, shoving outstretched hands in front of him to congratulate the day's hero.

"That was some throw," exclaimed one of the gray squirrels. "Think you could teach some of *us* to chuck like that?"

Ross smiled at the newfound admiration. *How quickly the tables had turned.* "I'll see what I can do."

***

Across the meadow from the raucous forest party, deep in the base of the mountain range, Kilgore and her cubs were settling into the cave for the night.

The grizzly was in pain from her antler wounds. She paced around the cave, trying to find a comfortable spot to lay, but to no avail. The cubs had already chosen their spot together in the back, against the far wall.

"Comfortable, boys?" Kilgore asked sarcastically.

"Yep," said Arnold innocently.

"How about you," replied Wesley, almost as if on cue.

"If I was *comfortable*, I wouldn't be pacing around, *would* I," snapped Kilgore, momentarily agitated by the dull pain of her injuries.

"Mom," Arnold whined, completely oblivious to her state of mind, "I'm hungry."

"Me too," Wesley chimed in.

Stiff and sore, she ambled to the corner and near her boys. She circled the spot and then laid her weary body down.

The ground was hard, but it felt sublime to rest. Kilgore was in more pain than she wanted to let on to the boys, always striving to perpetuate a courageous demeanor. It was her deepest desire to inspire them to become mentally tough, just like her.

She tried to relax, but the cubs moaned. Stomachs grumbled and gurgled, echoing off the cave walls, thwarting her concentrated effort to forget about the injuries and her own starvation.

She looked over at her boys and lowered her head to the ground.

She felt their hunger.

Kilgore was old, and the years in the Rocky Mountains were tough on her mind and body.

She didn't blame them for complaining, frankly. Some days, she wanted to complain, too, but she wanted to set an example for them.

Today, however, she felt she had failed them in the meadow.

Times weren't always this hard. For years, the mountainous region she'd migrated from provided a rich bounty of animals, fish, and fruit. Elk, deer, and moose grazed below her childhood home as far as her honey-brown eyes could see. Plentiful antelope roamed wild, ripe for the picking at just about any time. Whole *herds* of them. Jackrabbits and badgers roamed the cliff's face in quick-spawned abundance.

Kilgore never had a problem providing for herself in those days, but over the last year or two since the boys were born, the prey had disappeared from the miles of bountiful land she called home.

She was forced to move on.

Forced to *adapt*.

That was the reason she'd come to the rocky range overlooking the area others called the Great Timbers. Suddenly, she found herself plunged into a steep and sprawling landscape filled with enough live prey to raise *ten* cubs on.

But, today, she had overestimated her abilities, and the boys were paying for her mistakes.

Kilgore stared at Arnold and Wesley, her brilliant-eyed boys who were only a year apart and nearly shared a mind. They lay clutching each other in a loving, brotherly embrace.

She thought back to a time just a few short years ago when she and Brutus, their late father, shared an intimate closeness, snuggling for warmth and hibernating through devastating Wyoming winters together.

She missed having him as a steady rock to lean on and was sad that the boys would have to grow up without him. She often found herself trying to be stronger than she actually was to create the kind of influence Brutus would have had he not been taken from them all.

It was time to face reality. The season would change soon, and she was determined to ensure that her boys were taken care of for the freezing season that lay ahead. They needed full bellies to hibernate. They needed fat reserves to survive until the spring, a time she imagined would be just as stunning as autumn in this new rocky range.

As the moon subtly shifted beyond the mouth of the cave and the chill fell upon them, Kilgore thought about the smell she'd picked up on in the meadow. The one that broke her concentration and made her flee with the children to safety.

It was an *unnatural* smell.

Unlike any animal, foul scat, or decomposition she'd ever crossed paths with in the Rockies. Something *smoky* and *odorous*. Noxious scents that were carried through the air on the strong western winds.

Regardless, she should've finished what she started.

If not for her, then for the *boys*.

Kilgore lay there in the dark of the cave as the faint light of distant stars made ominous silhouettes of the scraggly pines beyond.

Tomorrow, she decided with conviction, *we feast.*

11

Mickey sat up in his cot and put on his boots while the other men were fast asleep in the wee hours of the morning. He grabbed the case to his rifle and silently took the weapon out. He returned the case to the spot beneath his cot in an attempt to not arouse any unnecessary suspicion. It would only weigh him down.

Anything he needed, he could re-purchase eventually. The case, his clothes... they were all replaceable. After he bagged either his elk or bear without a tag, and after Notches found the unfortunate cannon fodder he'd kicked under the juniper, Mickey would surely be on Notches's mental wanted list.

He slung the rifle's strap across his shoulder and grabbed the zippered shoulder-pack he'd loaded with ammunition, elk calls, binoculars, a headlamp, a hunting knife, and the remnants of his flask of whiskey.

He stealthily made his way to the tent flap, looked back to ensure he wasn't forgetting anything vital, then walked out into the darkness, leaving the others behind.

Quite possibly forever.

***

Mickey hiked towards the ridge, using only the faint beam of his nearly-drained headlamp to make his way up the twisted trail. He cursed beneath his breath over the loss of the map, a discovery he'd made along the trek. He was unsure where he could've misplaced it.

As he walked cautiously along the path, the headlamp blinked off, then on again. He smacked the device with his numbed fingertips, and it illuminated the path again. He let out a sigh of relief, watching his breath fog the air in front of him.

A few steps further, the light blinked off again.

Mickey smacked it harder, whispering his curses louder, but the light didn't come on this time.

He had to be careful. One wrong move, one awkward step, one slippery footing… and injury was highly probable.

He took a step.

Then another.

He felt around the hard earth with his boots, reaching out for branches and trunks to grasp as he made his way up the treacherous slope.

BAM!

"God--"

He tripped over a downed tree branch that had fallen across the narrow path and slammed, gloved palms first, against the ground with a muffled thud. His bruised knees hit the packed soil, and he yowled in pain, covering his mouth almost immediately with a hand.

Stupid, stupid, stupid, he thought.

Want to run off all the elk and bear, you idiot? Why don't you just send Jimmy and Notches a beacon pointing right where you are?!

Angry and unable to see the path, he sat on a rotting log and dusted the dirt from his camouflaged pants. He yanked off his useless headlamp and chucked it into the woods in frustration.

He put a cigarette between his lips but refused to light it, knowing that the scent would surely kill all chances of getting within range of either of the prized mammals he had on his mind. Still, pinching it between his lips soothed him.

Mickey took the 30-06 Springfield and pack off his shoulders, and rested them against the log. He touched the cool metal barrel, marveling at the beautiful, man-made creation. It was black as crushed velvet with a smooth bolt-action, topped with a modest 3-9 scope. It was nothing fancy. Nothing like the gun he'd bought for Jimmy all those years ago. But it certainly did the job. Months back, he'd purchased it from a gunsmith in Casper, hoping that someday he'd find large game worth firing at.

Finally, he *had*.

As he waited for the sky to lighten just enough to continue his journey, the memory of the elk and grizzly brought the hint of a smile to the corners of his chapped lips.

12

The light of dawn washed the Great Timbers in a dull, blue glow by the time Big Bob finally awoke. He lay there on the bed of leaves tucked into the woods beyond the forested treeline of the meadow.

The pain in his shoulder had been somewhat eased by the herbal poultice. He was stiff and sore, mouth parched.

Careful not to awaken the yearlings, Big Bob rose and made his way through the tall grass field. He bee-lined for the small stream on the far edge, desperately wanting to quench his thirst with fresh, running water.

He studied the nearly silent serenity of the area he called home and carefully stepped into the cold liquid so as not to disturb Richard's slumber. He bowed his head for a sip and chewed at the tall, delicious grass along the water's edge. He could feel a small amount of his strength returning with every bite.

Just ahead, at the edge of the tree line, was a pair of assessing eyes in the darkness. Oblivious to the danger, Big Bob continued to chew as the hulking mass lumbered toward him, its steps drowned out by the gentle trickle of the stream.

Kilgore roared, a sound that echoed through the meadow, waking the others and turning the blood coursing through Big Bob's body into ice.

She clicked all five of her terrifying claws against the face of the rock in front of her, one lining the stream that narrowly separated the foes.

She stepped out of the shadowy treeline into the early morning rays of sun sneaking through the birches and pines.

"Ain't *this* nice, boys?" She sneered and licked her lips as Arnold and Wesley crept out of the shadows behind her, both expressions impossible to decipher.

"Breakfast came to *us*."

13

Just as daylight tickled its finger-like rays across the Great Timbers, a clear hissing noise awoke Notches from his slumber. He sat bolt-upright in his cot and listened to the soft, sorrow-filled yowls emanating from outside.

Notches reached over to the adjacent cot and shook Jimmy fervently. "Jim, wake up."

Jimmy groaned and rolled over, batting the sleep from his puffy eyes. The morning air was frigid, and he wrapped the sleeping bag tighter around himself.

Roooooooooooooooooo!

The soft cry came from just outside the tent.

Jimmy shrugged and blinked a few times, "That a *coyote*?"

"Naw." Notches shook his head, listened intently, and then scrambled for his boots.

Jimmy sat up, still dazed. His gaze fell to the empty cot. "Where's Mickey?"

"Dunno. Don't rightly care, either, if I'm bein' honest." Notches was preoccupied. He picked up his rifle, checked the chamber, then slammed the bolt closed. He then threw on his boots, leaving them unlaced, and shuffled out the flap of the tent.

Once outside, he stood still for a moment until the next pitiful wail sounded off into the cold morning air. Notches whipped his head toward the source and headed straight toward it, gun readied, barrel pointed at a nearby bush.

"*Keeka*?" Notches's voice was nearly a whisper. He stared at a thick hedge of juniper bushes just beyond the treeline, "That you, girl?"

As he approached the trees, the whine turned into a pathetic, high-pitched whimper.

He followed it slowly and used the barrel of the rifle to make a gap in the dense, rubbery branches to see inside.

There was his wolfdog.

His costly little pride and joy...

She was lying on her side, squirming in the dirt.

"What in the *world*?" Notches lowered to his knees next to the dog and placed his weapon on the ground. He slid her out from beneath the bush, watching her head loll awkwardly as if in a daze.

"What *happened* to you, girl?!"

He knew she couldn't answer but couldn't stop himself from asking.

His forehead wrinkled, and his thin lips frowned. Panic swelled inside him as he checked her for claw marks and defensive wounds.

The *smell*…

What was that *smell*?

Notches sniffed around and lowered his head to the dog. The smell was potent there.

Kerosene.

It was unmistakable, and the bandanna was soaked with it. He tugged the rag from around her neck and held it, disgusted.

Did she drink it?

Was the dog dumb enough to lap up kerosene, he wondered. *Where was her tracking collar?*

None of it made sense.

Keeka whined and yipped. Raising her head seemed to be an exhaustive effort.

Notches looked around and thought for a moment. Being so deep in the woods, it would be hours before he could get her to a veterinarian.

That kind of suffering was inhumane.

As much as it pained him to lose a trained -- and *expensive* -- dog, he imagined he was going to have to put her out of her misery.

Notches tossed the knotted loop of fabric down with an infuriated groan and made another discovery in the dawning light:

A folded piece of paper, mostly buried under a dense layer of pine needles.

He unfolded it to reveal a hand-drawn map of the mountain range nearby. He recognized the paper and the messy scrawled images and the chicken-scratch handwriting on it.

Mickey.

Rage surged through him. The pieces tumbled into place in his mind. He grasped the map as hard as he wanted to grasp Mickey's *throat*, burying his own dirty nails into his palm so hard he thought it might bleed.

The dog whined again, and Jimmy crept up behind them with trepidation.

"Good lord, what'd she do? Tangle with somethin' big?"

"Yeah," Notches gritted his teeth and tensed his jaw until it was hard as steel, locking his moss-green eyes on Keeka, "somethin' about five-foot-four and a hundred an' twenty pounds."

14

By the time the morning sun breached the top of the colossal pines, Mickey arrived at a boulder-filled section of mountain near the ridge. He cursed himself for losing the map but felt momentary pride when he found the familiar area from memory.

He stepped onto a large boulder at the edge of the steep path and eyed the sheer, deadly drop-off in front of him. His body tensed with fear. He then glanced up, studying the meadow below, and managed a smile.

Mickey adjusted the rifle strap on his aching shoulder and continued up the rocky slope towards the ridge where he'd seen the bear and elk the afternoon prior.

****

Keeka lethargically followed Jimmy and Notches through the dense woods, eyes still struggling to stay open as she walked.

Notches stopped and looked at the hand-drawn map. Jimmy craned his neck over Notches's shoulder and stared at it, too. The men looked up the trail, then back down the slope.

"Are we on the right track?" Jimmy asked.

Notches didn't respond right away.

Instead, his eyes locked onto something ten feet away, in the leaves up ahead. Something the color of a faded marigold. He lowered the folded paper and stalked toward it.

Jimmy watched him carefully, curious to see what had caught the man's eye.

"Yup. We're on the right trail," his voice soft, confident.

"How do you know?"

Notches held up the butt of one of Mickey's cigarettes.

"It's his brand."

15

Mickey watched the second-round interaction with his binoculars, perched on a flat-topped boulder on the ridge. His heart raced as he locked his gaze on the massive bull elk at the edge of the meadow. With just a slight twitch of his hands, he could see the bear. There, across the stream from the bull, stood the mammoth grizzly.

He couldn't believe his good fortune.

To see both creatures again a day later? Sure, it was bizarre, but Mickey didn't give the rarity of it much thought. The only thing running through his head was the question of which animal he wanted mounted in his den more.

The grizzly? Or the elk?

Eenie-meenie…Miney-moe…

Decisions, decisions.

Mickey snickered as he looked at the two magnificent animals in his scope but was interrupted by the crunch of dry leaves behind him. Just as he started to turn around, he felt a hard *slam* into the back of his head.

Everything went black.

***

Notches stood over Mickey's limp body, rifle in hand. "That's for my dog!"

He raised his boot and kicked the unconscious old man in the ribs.

Mickey lay there, unconscious in the dirt, just as the canine had.

"This is a nice little spot ya' found here, Mickey." Notches tried to smile with his slight underbite, looking out over the forest and meadow with his atrocious posture, but the expression came off as more of a grimace.

He stepped over Mickey's unconscious body to the rocky edge and glanced out over the beautiful meadow. He raised the 300 Winchester Magnum to his face and stared through his scope at the stirring commotion at the far end of the meadow's treeline.

Huffing and wheezing, Jimmy made his way through the clearing in the trees and saw Mickey lying on the ground. His smile fell, and a look of horror spread across his face.

Notches seemed oblivious, peering out into the meadow, chuckling. "Ah, 'at's what you was after, Mick!"

16

There was nowhere to go. The elk was certain he wouldn't outrun her, or worse, she'd attack the others nearby, like his son. Without any further warning, Big Bob lurched forward, galloping fast. An attack now would be the only way to take the bear even slightly off-guard.

The bull lowered his head and charged at the bear, digging his hooves deep into the squishy stream's bank. He plunged his rack into Kilgore, pushing with all the strength his sore shoulders could muster.

Kilgore roared with ferocity as the animal smashed into her bruised chest, tearing new holes with the points of his horns.

Just then, a sound rang out through the Great Timbers.

BOOM!

All the birds in the trees scattered wildly into the air. Deer skittered into the forest. Richard dunked his head beneath the water of the stream. The foreign sound was terrifying, but no one could comprehend its source.

Kilgore looked at Big Bob, still locked in the bear's death grip. The bull writhed and squirmed in place, harder now, trying to escape instead of attack.

Kilgore held tight, and Big Bob's legs flailed and skidded awkwardly beneath him, eyes wide with horror. The bear wrestled his large form, and the elk went down hard. She saw blood on his side and was confused. It wasn't an area she remembered clawing…

The elk's eyes fluttered back, the once tense muscles relaxed. The formidable prey no longer struggled against Kilgore's unbreakable grasp. The great timbers had lost its mighty enforcer. Big Bob's once-strong, massive body turned limp in her paws.

BOOM!

Another shot.

This time, something struck Kilgore in the flesh of her belly. The bear thrashed backward, releasing Big Bob's body, and dropped hard to the ground. She rolled on her rounded back from the piercing pain and sudden impact.

Big Bob dropped to the ground, uncoordinated legs trying to find purchase. Mouth gasping for air. The look on his face was one of shock and terror.

Ryan galloped up to Big Bob as soon as they heard the shot.

"What happened? Dad, get up! *Please*, get up! We have to get you out of here before Kilgore--"

Kilgore scrambled to her back feet and stumbled back into the line of colossal pines, where her sons had viewed the ordeal.

Kilgore stumbled up the hill. As the obedient cubs headed up the path, following close behind, Kilgore turned toward Ryan and the others in the meadow. She sniffed the air and then roared:

"Run! Run as fast as you can! Humans are near!" Blood rolled down her shaking legs. With that, she turned and galloped up the tree-studded mountain toward her cave, leaving a ruby trail along the way.

"Humans?" Ryan asked with horrified confusion. His father's eyes weren't connecting with his. They were staring downstream into nothingness. "What's a human? What's she talking about? Dad!"

"Ryan, we have to go!" Edward squealed.

"I can't leave him here!" Ryan cried and pleaded, "Dad, *please* get up!"

The others stood in shock, forming a semi-circle at the edge of the woods, all staring at their fallen leader from what they perceived as a safe distance.

Big Bob's gaze was fixed. His chest stopped expanding. He lay there near the stream, lifeless.

Ryan stared down at Big Bob's stilled body as waves of horror and sorrow flooded over him.

"Get up, Dad!" Ryan wept, his shaking voice now coming out in melancholic bleats.

Bob Bob didn't budge.

Edward and some of the sows from the harem crept out from the treeline and joined Ryan.

The bull's body was still in the shadow of those he swore to his *own father*, long ago, that he would protect.

Ryan looked down to the dark, maned chest of long hair that once moved with breath and life…

To the mighty rack worn like a regal crown upon his father's head. To eyes wide and unblinking, filled with shock.

It was at that moment he realized that his father would never get up again.

17

When Jimmy heard the first shot from the rifle, he nearly dropped Mickey's binoculars. The blast was unexpected, and he'd watched as the elk was struck.

"What are you doing?!" Jimmy looked up just in time to see his friend reloading. "Notches, we don't have a tag for that!"

Keeka took off like a rocket, scurrying away from the source of the sound, disappearing down the tree-lined dirt path toward the meadow far below.

"What are you doing?! Are you out of your mind?" Jimmy hollered, stepping toward the armed man, voice echoing down through the vast expanse beyond. He could feel his pulse in his throat.

"Elk aren't in season yet! You don't even have a tag for that! That's a $50,000 fine! You could get a year in *prison!*"

Notches ignored Jimmy, taking aim again, narrowing his eyes to stare through the barrel of the scope.

"Are you *insane*, Nick? You already hit it."

"I hit the elk." He paused and sniggered, "I've never seen a grizzly, Jim. And I don't reckon I might ever see one again."

"Not at *this* rate. Because we'll be locked up in *Rawlins*, you idiot!"

Notches lifted his face away from the scope and smiled at Jimmy. "Good thing I got me a good lawyer, then."

He winked and returned his gaze to the grizzly. "Imagine how many rich idiots you'll be bringing to the *Elk Mountain Lodge* next year when they see 'ese mounts on the website. Pretty sure I'm doing you a *favor*, Jimbo."

With that...

Notches fired again.

18

Keeka ran across the meadow as fast as she could, timidly approaching the gathering of woodland animals surrounding the downed elk. She barked loud and frantic.

Coming down the ridge, Notches and Jimmy heard her and smiled.

"Atta girl!" Notches smiled, thrilled that the dog was doing what she'd been trained to do: aid his efforts in tracking game.

But Keeka wasn't tracking the kill.

She was warning the others.

***

Keeka raced over to the yearlings, already mourning the loss of their leader. Her head hung low with reverence and sympathy.

She wanted to apologize for her master. *But it would be a waste of valuable time,* she thought.

Normally, the presence of her frightened away woodland creatures. In the past, most have gone skittering away at the sight of her.

But not these.

These animals stayed in place.

Unfazed.

Shaken and in shock by the horrific event they had all just bore witness to. Everyone was still trying to make sense of the tragedy, each unsure of what had transpired.

"You've got to go," Keeka barked. "You've all got to go *right now!* The humans! They're coming this way! *Please*," she begged.

Ryan lifted his heartbroken, watery gaze from the body of his father and looked to Keeka. There was that strange word again.

Humans.

"Who *are* you," he asked, eyes blurred with tears.

"My name is Keeka. I'm sorry, but there's no time for pleasantries right now. You *have* to get out of here, or you'll end up the same as him!"

"Who... *did* this?" Ryan asked, ignoring the order, mind in a daze.

"*They* did!" She motioned with a whip of her head, still barking at the top of her lungs in between exhausted pants. "The humans. *My* human."

Ryan looked in the direction she'd pointed, watching the trees sway in the wind. The camouflage-covered two-legged creatures stumbled down the winding path from the mountains.

Humans.

Creatures that walked on their hind legs and carried boom-sticks, just as his father had said in the dark corner of the forest the night before.

The word was as surreal and bizarre as the situation Ryan found himself in, like some awful nightmare he couldn't seem to shake.

"They're coming for *him*." Keeka's azure-blue eyes dropped to Big Bob, and then she turned away immediately, wondering if she might be sick. She wanted to chew some grass but knew there was no time. "They'll do this to *you*, too, if they get the chance. I'm sure of it!"

Ryan lifted his head and looked at the creatures around him. He needed to act fast.

It's what his father would have wanted him to do. It's what the bull would have done *himself.*

"Everyone, seek shelter. *Now!*" Ryan commanded. His small, bleating voice had the squelch of unfathomable pain in every syllable. "You all must hide until the threat is gone. I'll bugle when it's safe." He took a moment, trying not to break down, and then lifted his head again and cleared his throat. "Don't come out until then, *please!*"

The creatures slowly broke away from the gathered mob and scattered throughout the meadow, as far as their legs and wings would take them, picking up speed the further they traveled from the downed elk.

The wolfdog started to trot away when Ryan bleated again.

"Keeka?"

She stopped in her tracks and looked over her tufted, tri-color shoulder at him, light eyes gleaming in the sun.

"*Thank you,*" Ryan said with sincerity, gritting his molars, muscles tense.

Keeka offered a half-nod and then took off at full speed toward the trail up the mountain.

19

Storm clouds gradually settled over the distant peaks, and the temperature of the air started to drop, almost as if the mountain was angered by the scene below.

Mickey was coming around. He lay there on the hard ground, trying to focus his eyes, and finally sat up, noticing blood on his flannel shirt. His head pounded.

He looked around for his Springfield. The rifle was gone. All he found was a handful of spent cartridges on the ground, rolling gently back and forth with the whipping of the icy wind. He picked some up and chucked them over the edge of the treacherous ridge in anger. He growled and pounded a fist on the dry dirt.

Notches and Jimmy.

Had to be, he thought.

Although, the restraint Notches showed in not killing him was a surprise. The man was untethered and wild, capable of truly dark deeds. The fact that Mickey was only bleeding and unconscious, and not *dead,* was nothing short of a miracle.

He stood up, aggressively dusted himself off, and stalked back to camp with revenge on his mind.

***

Deep in the forest, many of the animals had gathered in private huddles of grief and sorrow. Other woodland creatures watched the humans approach their fallen king from spots they deemed safe, like high boughs of nearby trees.

An owl soared overhead, giving some of the others updates on the strange hind-leg creature's whereabouts.

From a spot beyond the meadow, behind a downed trunk wedged between some thick trees and brush, Ryan's eyes swelled with tears as he watched the two far-away humans approach his father.

Ross, however, was unfortunate enough to be close to the men, having never left the tree he'd climbed that morning. He'd witnessed the fight and subsequent atrocity from a high branch in a nearby birch bordering the stream. Being only a short distance away, he'd seen far too much already.

He could still imagine Kilgore limping clumsily up the path to her mountain cave with her terrified cubs in tow.

He could see Big Bob, too, still as a boulder beside the stream where he'd perished.

Ross watched the two strange-looking humans closely.

***

Notches whipped Mickey's Springfield off his shoulder and lobbed it into the grass beside the kill. He held out his Win-Mag and tugged the fixed-blade hunting knife out of its sheath on his belt. Beaming with pride, he carved another notch into the walnut stock.

"Notch your gun later!" Jimmy growled. "We have to get this out of here, *fast*! I am not going down for this, you hear me?"

He paced up and down the length of the animal, heart racing with the fear of getting caught.

Still, as a hunter himself, he marveled at the sheer size of Notches's prize.

"I'll *hurry*. Don't get yer panties in a twist, Jimbo." Notches rolled his eyes, and something caught his attention:

A raccoon kit, up in the nearby tree.

The mammal stared down at him, unintentionally chattering with fear and grief.

"Whatchu lookin' at, you lil trash-eater," he grimaced and then spit into the grass, never taking his hooded, green eyes off the animal.

"What are you worryin' about a raccoon for? Do what you need to *do*, or I'm getting in the side-by-side and leaving you out here."

Notches whipped around, pointed the sharpened knife like a finger, and flashed a venomous glare at his boss. "You wouldn't *dare*."

After a moment of tension, Notches squatted down and expertly cut into the animal with the tools from the 3-piece field kit strapped to his hip. He snickered as he cut, singing in an attempt to lighten the tone. "*Jimmy cracked horns, and I don't care… Jimmy cracked horns, and I don't care--*"

"Shut up. Okay? Stop… *singing*. Just shut up and cut."

"Aww, c'mon, Jimmy-Joe, *relax*! We've been out here for *days,* and we ain't seen not-a one game warden in all 'at time. So jus', take a deep breath and think about how sweet this thing's gonna look on the wall 'a the *Elk Mountain Lodge* when it's built."

Jimmy cracked half a smile. "You're not lyin'. Can't *believe* the size of the rack on that thing." His smile fell. "How are we gonna get that out of here without being seen? This was just a *scout*, man. I wasn't prepared for any of this. Those horns are *massive*. They're not gonna fit in my SUV, and it's not like we can just strap those on the *roof*."

Notches grinned wide. "I already thought'a that."

He reached into the pocket of his camo pants and pulled out a set of keys, holding them up on his blood-covered index finger.

"We're takin' *Mickey's* ride. After he tried to kill my dog, the *least* he could do's loan us the truck."

"He'll call the cops and report it stolen."

Notches went back to cutting, slicing through meat and tendon, then pulling out his serrated bone saw. "I don't know about *you,* but…"

He looked back over his shoulder again with another wicked smile. "I ain't had a single bar 'a service since I been out here."

Jimmy nodded.

It was a valid point.

None of them had.

Cell towers in Wyoming were few and far between, even wider-spread in vast expanses of wilderness and mountains like this.

"I don't know about all this, Nick."

Notches stopped cutting and pinched his eyes closed in frustration. Jimmy almost never called him by his real name.

"It'll be *fine*, Jimmy. Look, we'll throw the grizzly in with it and tuck both under the tarp, then keep it down with coolers and tie-downs and stuff. We'll come back out for the tent and all the rest later." He giggled. "Heck, maybe Mickey too, if 'at moron's had enough time to sit and think about what he done."

"Yeah, but Nick, what if we get stopped without a tag--"

Notches whipped around and pointed the glinting edge of the gut-hook knife again.

"I swear if you whine about 'at tag *one more time…*"

Notches didn't finish the sentence. He pursed his lips and looked down at the grass. He itched his face with the back of his arm, accidentally smearing a streak of red up his stubbled jawline.

"It's gonna be alright. You're panickin' about nothin'."

Jimmy swallowed hard. It didn't matter that the man was his employee. The guy was unhinged.

Psychotic.

After seeing him attack Mickey earlier with such remorseless ease, he knew Notches was capable of further carefree violence.

Notches went back to cutting.

Jimmy looked around, affixing his gaze on something a few feet away. "Looks like the bear took off this way." He pointed at the sanguine trail leading up the steep slope of the mountain.

He walked over to the elk, bent down, and grabbed Notches's Win-Mag.

Notches slammed his glistening hand down on top of Jimmy's, smashing it against the gun and smearing it red.

"What do you think you're *doin'*?" Notches glared with fury in his eyes.

Jimmy stared down at their hands, enamored by the shine of the blood the crazed man had imprinted onto his skin.

"I-I was just… in case the bear isn't *dead*. You don't want somethin' that big, injured, and pissed-off springing out at us while you're cuttin' that bull up, do you?"

Notches thought for a moment and nodded with reluctance. With trepidation, he grabbed the Win-Mag by the barrel and hoisted it in the air as an offering.

Jimmy snatched up the smeared gun and checked the chamber to ensure it was, in fact, loaded. Once satisfied, he stared off into the direction of the spatter, readied. He watched the timberline nervously and then peered up at the darkening sky, swallowing hard.

He shivered as the cold wind blasted through his woodland camo sweatshirt. "Let's hurry it up. Weather looks like it's about to get ugly, and you still have a bear to find."

20

Mickey arrived back at the campsite about the time the cloud cover darkened the land in a thick, nearly opaque sheet. The stormy sky had changed astonishingly quick.

Once inside, Mickey rubbed his hands together to warm them and scanned the tent to make sure he was alone. He shivered, still furious about his missing rifle as well as the truck keys that had been in his pocket. He kicked his pack of gear into the canvas side of the tent with a grunt. It was the only thing his assailant left behind.

His head was throbbing. It was a constant, thudding reminder of the revenge he now sought.

He made his way over to the kerosene heater in the middle of the tent and clicked it on, holding his papery hands near it.

Once warmed, he lowered himself onto his cot, reached into the kangaroo pouch of his camouflaged hoodie, and pulled a cigarette out. He lit it, took a deep drag, and exhaled.

***

Keeka watched Mickey through the ajar flap of the tent, and all of the memories from the night before came rushing back to her, like a vehicle with no brakes slamming into her full force.

The *red rag.*

That *smell.*

The awful man leaving her discarded there, tucked beneath some bushes like wind-swept trash.

He'd pay for what he'd done to her.

She looked around the tent at the coolers and camping gear. Suddenly, her blue eyes caught sight of the bottle of kerosene Mickey had doused her neck scarf with.

The cap was still off.

The wafting smell burned her nose with its all-too-familiar scent, reminding her of the night before in traumatically vivid detail. She didn't want to get anywhere near the noxious smell, but she had to make sure that Mickey could never hurt her, *or any other animals for that matter*, ever again.

She clamped her powerful jaw around the handle of the jug and tugged the bottle around the corner through the dirt.

Mickey heard rustling and reached for his gun, surprised, yet again, to find it wasn't strapped across his shoulders. He felt naked without it.

He knew that the sound was most likely Notches, toying with him before another assault.

Frankly, he was surprised the psycho didn't kill him on the mountain. But this time, he had the element of surprise. He crept closer to the noise on the other side of the canvas…

Keeka stopped halfway to the back and nudged the jug with her snout until it was pressed against the fabric wall and then nudged again. It fell on its side. Kerosene glugged out, flowing freely down the canvas tent material along the dirt slope beneath the tent, puddling near the foot of the unsuspecting hunter's cot.

The moment that Mickey dropped his lit cigarette butt on the ground, he knew he had made a mistake.

In a flash, the ground was ablaze.

Flames woofed up his dust-covered pant legs. He let out a scream that rose up from the toes of his now flaming, mud-encrusted boots. The fire licked higher to his thighs. He slapped them with his hands in a panic, unsure of what to do.

He flailed and fell against the nearby wall of the tent, and the flames caught that, too. He tripped over his overturned gear pack and slammed it onto the ground, which soaked him in more kerosene and made the fire exponentially worse. Mickey fought to get to his feet.

The hot, orange tendrils consumed the tent like greedy, grabbing hands grasping for anything they could for consumption.

Mickey dragged himself outside and rolled in the dirt, trying to extinguish the active flames. *Stop, drop, and roll,* the frantic thought chirped in his mind from his younger school days. He did just that, rolling in the dirt, trying to pat it all out with the dusty Wyoming soil.

He looked around for Jimmy and Notches and found himself alone…

Well, almost.

Before him sat the calm, lone wolfdog, the one with the dusty red handkerchief he'd tried to kill her with still tied around her thick neck.

They locked eyes.

"What the…?" He growled in pain.

Keeka's blue eyes narrowed. She bared her fangs.

And *charged.*

Keeka hurled her body straight onto the still-smoking menace before her.

Mickey raised his charred hands to protect himself from his fur-covered attacker.

The forceful impact of the wolfdog knocked him back into the still-burning canvas, slamming his frail spine hard into the arid ground. She tore into his throat, sinking into the squishy meat. She shook her head hard, imagining him as small prey whose neck would be malleable enough to *shake and kill.*

He tried to scream, but with the damage done to his throat, the sound came out as a gurgling wheeze.

She stepped back and licked the pink from her lips.

Mickey choked and sizzled in agony, one hand around his throat, as the fire consumed him. He inched his burning body towards the animal and swiped.

The wolfdog took a few careful steps back to avoid his flailing grasp.

After a moment, Mickey lost the fight, and his bizarre gamut of noises stopped.

She stood there, from a safe distance, watching. As the old man perished, the smell of smoke crept into her already-stinging sinuses.

21

Clouds hung heavy over the forest with the approaching storm, echoing the gloomy sentiments of the recent tragedy across the land. As he trekked into the woods, Ross saw the other animals waiting for him just beyond the grassy meadow.

His darkened mind swirled with thoughts about telling the others what he had seen...

What they'd done to Big Bob.

His face echoed the utter shock from images that replayed on a horrendous loop in his fragile mind.

Seeing the distress in his wide eyes, Heather approached. Normally jovial, her smile had completely vanished, and her fluffy tail lay limply on the ground behind her. "Ross, what did those *things* want?"

Ross stared into Heather's concerned face and then cast his gaze somberly back down at the ground.

He spoke softly, unable to answer her question. He didn't understand it at all. "Can you gather the animals for a meeting? Especially the birds, squirrels, and other raccoons. Richard, too. Bring everyone. Could you do that for me?"

She nodded. "Of course. What about the elk and deer? And *Ryan*? Do you want me to get him too?" Heather bit her lower lip to keep from crying.

"No!" His eyes were large and panicked behind the dark fur mask, petrified of having to explain to everyone what he'd seen, especially to Big Bob's *son*.

"Please," his hands raised, tiny fingers splayed, "find a way to keep Ryan away. Ask Edward to stay with him. Don't let him go anywhere near the other side of the meadow until I have a chance to talk to the others. I don't want him to see."

"Okay." Heather sensed the urgency in Ross's voice. She nodded and scurried toward the others as fast as her swift little legs could carry her.

At the edge of the meadow, Ross looked up at the clouds, ominous and threatening, wishing they would open up and wash away the memories of what he had just witnessed.

22

Jimmy started the three-quarter-mile trek back up to get the side-by-side while Notches left the head of the bull to find and field-dress the grizzly. He saw splashes of burgundy with nearly every step, drying to the color of rust, trailing along the mountainside.

He didn't have to go far before he found the bear face down in the dirt beneath a tree with two trembling cubs by the stump behind her.

As soon as Notches came into view, the cubs scattered into the trees, hesitant to leave their mother but frightened of the man in camo.

The mother was clearly dead, still as a downed tree, but Notches pointed the gun at her anyway, just in case.

He kicked her back foot with his shoe, and it wiggled lifelessly from the momentum of his own foot. He nudged her leg with the barrel of his Win-Mag and let out an elated sigh of relief and joy.

Without a word, he went to work dismantling the beast, carefully removing the hide and skull as he had done to hundreds of animals before.

23

As he turned the corner at the top of the path, Jimmy saw black smoke rising from the direction of the tent and picked up his pace. As he burst through the last remnants of the tree line, he saw what was left of the campsite…

Still smoldering.

Jimmy's mouth hung open in shock as he watched the last flames flicker out. He scrambled out of the truck and walked closer to the charred mess. He reflexively covered his nose to protect against the horrid smell of burning hair.

Kneeling beside him, Jimmy took in the horrifying image of Mickey's burned body. With the barrel of the rifle in his hands, he rolled the grotesque form over to see that it was, in fact, Mickey. Jimmy rushed over to the junipers and threw up into the bushes.

***

Who did this?

Who could…?

How…?

Jimmy's frantic brain swirled a million thoughts as he stared at Mickey with a hand covering his mouth.

Now, it wasn't just poaching that Jimmy was worried about.

The $100,000.00 in possible fines and two years of prison time for the grizzly and elk *paled* in comparison to the charges that Notches and he might now face.

Arson.

Assault.

Murder. (Or at least *manslaughter.*)

And if they left now, trying to skirt it all, possibly even *obstruction of justice.*

Now, the scramble to load up Mickey's pickup truck was on.

But what if Mickey was found and his vehicle was in their possession? They would look even more suspicious.

He fished the keys for the side-by-side out of his pocket, wedged himself inside the vehicle, and took off down the winding path of the mountain toward Notches. He drove as fast as he could without driving off the steep side of the slope into the deadly canyon below.

The clock was ticking.

***

The twenty minutes it took to get to Notches and explain what happened felt like an eternity to Jimmy. His nerves were shot. He was sure they would be arrested, sure he could kiss all hopes of opening the *Elk Mountain Lodge* goodbye forever. He'd be too busy counting his pennies for the prison commissary to rake in any rich-yuppie dough with a lodge.

Once back at the ashen campsite, Jimmy slung Mickey's rifle into the beat-up truck bed and raced off into the junipers again to vomit.

Notches examined the body of his acquaintance with curiosity and no hint of remorse.

"I always told him smoking'd be the death of him." Notches cackled, calm and cool, as if nothing illegal had happened all day.

"What is wrong with you?" Jimmy wiped the bile from his lips, skin looking pallid and clammy. "The man is dead."

"Shoot, you're actin' like I killed him."

Jimmy just eyed him for a second. The thought hadn't occurred to him, but suddenly, it seemed plausible.

Notches took offense.

"Hey! I was with you all day! When would I have killed him?" He shook his head. "Here, I always thought you was the smart one of the three of us, what with your law degree and all. Sheesh." He looked Jimmy in the eye. "I had nothin' to do with this. I ain't exactly sad it *happened,* but I didn't do it, okay? The idiot probably did it to himself."

Jimmy wrapped his arms around his chest tight, paling at the sight of the body. "What do we do with him?"

Notches stood and craned his neck over to see Mickey's lower half. "Well, we could leave him. Coyotes and 'em cubs'd probably do the dirty work for us."

He thought for a moment. "Unless you got a shovel on you. Then we could bury him, I suppose."

"I didn't bring a shovel."

"Then I say we push him up under 'em bushes where he left my poor pup to rot. It'd serve the ol' fool right. 'At's karma, right there."

Without a better plan, Jimmy reluctantly agreed. They pulled Mickey's remains beneath the junipers and kicked a pile of pine needles on him.

They each grabbed one side of the elk's antlers and lifted the head into the truck bed with strained groans, carefully maneuvering it into the bed beneath the camper shell. Even separated from the rest of the animal, it was cumbersome.

"Heavy is the head that wears the crown," Notches joked, staring at the elk's massive rack of horns, narrowly fitting in the space. "*Sorry, not sorry.*" He snickered a little and grabbed the foot of the bear.

Jimmy didn't find the humor in any of it. He cringed at the thought of sharing the long ride back home with the deranged lunatic.

They tarped over the head of the elk and the shorn pelt and skull of the grizzly and jammed the tattered remnants of the tent and a few undamaged camping supplies in wherever they could make them fit.

They loaded the side-by-side onto the trailer, strapped it all down, and took off, Colorado-bound.

As they drove in silence, Jimmy wondered if he could sever ties if they somehow got out of this unscathed.

But, then again, he wondered if it was wiser to make nice with the man. Notches wasn't right in the head, and Jimmy didn't want to fall prey to the old adage:

Two can keep a secret… if one's dead.

24

As instructed, Heather gathered the animals together, all standing in a circle now, waiting for the raccoon to explain the purpose of the gathering.

Ross stepped up on a tree branch at the edge of the woods so they could all see him.

"What I'm about to say will be hard to hear. I will never be able to un-see the things I have seen today. We lost a great leader. Those *things--*"

"*Humans,*" one of the elder sows shouted from the back. "The wolf called them *humans.*"

"Yes, well." Ross tensed his narrow jaw. "Those *humans* murdered him."

Some elders and the harem erupted in a loud, squealing sob.

"Not for food, either," he added with disdain.

One of the young yearlings tried to bugle in disgust.

"Then… *why,*" cried Penelope, a black-and-white honey badger from the tall grass. Her three children were tucked in closely at her sides, faces reverent. "Why would anyone *do* such a thing?"

"Well," Ross stopped and looked at the glistening ground beneath them, alive with movement, as the beginning of the rain pattered gracefully through the grass.

He couldn't bring himself to tell the others of the atrocities he had just witnessed. The *thought* of telling them what the men did to the great elk made him feel sick.

He composed himself and looked at Heather's morose but beautiful face. He saw the sorrow she felt…

That they *all* felt.

"I honestly don't know why anyone would do… what they did." He swallowed hard. His throat felt like it was full of sand from the stream. "But I have gathered you because I think we should bury Big Bob. They dis… *dismantled* him." The word felt wrong in his mouth, but he didn't want to be more descriptive and frighten them further.

Several of the others gasped at the thought of it all.

"Ryan should never have to see his father in that condition. I say the young should keep Ryan away and occupied in the meantime."

"Anything for you, Ross," said one of the squirrels who had idolized the raccoon the evening prior for his bravery. "We're with you."

The other animals nodded solemnly.

The raccoon hung his head low. "I wanted to save him, but I--"

"There was nothing you could do. Nothing *any* of us could do, Ross," shouted a young doe named Kenna from behind. She cried. Her spotted back shuddered with the falling of her tears.

"Thank you." Ross cast his wide eyes to the ground, still horrified by the images living rent-free in his mind. He wondered how many times he would revisit the horrible sight at night when he closed his eyes to sleep. "Thank you all. We can work together and give him the burial he deserves. Something fit for a king."

The others dispersed in an orderly manner, and Ross climbed down from the branch.

He approached Heather, whose lovely eyes had grown red around the edges. He put his arm around her to comfort her, realizing quickly that it was him who actually needed it.

As Ross held her, he choked back his own tears, traumatized by the echoing memories of gleeful men desecrating the bull elk they had come to love and revere as their leader.

***

The badgers, weasels, and hedgehogs gathered sticks and brush throughout the soggy afternoon.

They packed them in bundles within the deer, elk, and antelope horns.

Later, the hawks and eagles plucked the bundles out, and, at the orchestration of the clever beaver, Richard, large families of chipmunks and squirrels arranged them carefully on and around their fallen leader. After that, a layer of pine needles and fallen leaves blanketed the top to fully obstruct Ryan's eyes from the state his father was in.

The animals worked tirelessly until Big Bob's desecrated and carelessly discarded remains were covered from view beneath a large burial mound.

The elk was laid to rest right where he perished.

Later, despite any differences they may have had at the start of the day, the community united as a family in their shared grief. They formed a circular mass around the grave site, with Ryan at the helm, each weeping over the loss of the beloved member who had long ago taken on the difficult responsibilities of leading them and keeping peace and order in a place that could quickly devolve into chaos.

Ryan stared at the mound, imagining his father laid to rest deep beneath it, wondering how this could all be, trying to wrap his mind around the life-altering events of the day.

One moment, Ryan was waking up to the sight of the mighty elk grazing near the stream's edge, majestic in the misty dawn of morning.

The next…

Big Bob was gone forever.

25

That evening, Arnold and Wesley walked, tumbled, and slid their way back down the steep path. With each step, the cubs, both hungry and heartbroken, made their way to the meadow, humbled by the situation.

Just as they stumbled out of the tree line, Ryan lifted his head high and narrowed his eyes, a sign of aggression despite his small stature.

"You're not welcome here! Haven't you all done *enough*," Ryan bleated angrily. "We've had enough devastation! Leave!"

The two cubs trembled, alone and despised, tears streaming down the wide curves of their young faces.

Ryan moved closer, then lowered his head as if to charge with his laughable spikes, brave despite the pain. "I said, be gone! *Now*!"

"But… we don't know where to go." Arnold's voice was small, frightened.

"Our *mother*," sobbed Wesley, "she--"

Arnold wrapped his arms around his younger brother in a loving bear hug.

Ryan's eyes grew wide. His expression softened. A pang of remorse choked the back of his throat. He knew from the agony in their cries, something which currently echoed his own distraught sentiments, that Kilgore was dead now, too.

His black eyes fixed on the burial mound, and he felt another swell of anger pulse through him. "If your mother hadn't come to the Great Timbers, none of this would have happened! You only want to *feed* on us. My father wouldn't have let it happen. Neither will *I*."

"That's not true," one of the sows interjected. She looked at the wailing cubs and then turned to Ryan. "A human did this. They are responsible for *all* of this."

"If not for those boom-sticks, their *mother* would have…" Ryan's voice cracked in frustration and pain. "He would have been in the same place he is now! That grizzly wouldn't have stopped until she got her way!"

"I'm sorry," Wesley squeaked from between his brother's arms. "She was just trying to *feed* us! We're *starving*! You must know what that's like."

But Ryan didn't.

He had been born unto a lush meadow, brimming with berries and tall grass, a luxury he wasn't even aware that he had until the boys said it.

In his short life, he'd never wanted for much beyond warmth.

"What is it you *want*," Ryan asked.

"Well, we were *hoping*," Arnold didn't know how to finish. He felt like a beggar.

Wesley spoke up, pulling out of his older brother's arms. "We were hoping that maybe you would take us in. Let us be part of your family."

"I understand why you wouldn't want to help us," Arnold said. "Trust me, I do." He offered his paws up in an act of submission. "It's just that… you all seem so healthy here. And we're all alone. We don't know what we are doing. We don't know the first thing about fending for ourselves."

"We'll die out there!" Tears streamed from Wesley's eyes.

That would serve you right, Ryan thought. But he didn't say it. The cruel response washed away like a bug on a fast-churning river.

Ryan paced.

His gut instinct was to send the bears away, even if it meant their death.

But, after today, Ryan realized that the meadow had suffered enough loss and devastation.

It seemed cruel to turn a blind eye on the begging young. At this rate, they might not even make it to winter if they were telling the truth about their starvation. He wrestled with the idea that they were still bears and that, even if they weren't lying now, someday they might turn out to be just as vicious as Kilgore.

Unsure if it would be wise or completely regrettable, he spoke, hoping his father would be proud. "I'll gather the others. Together, we will decide."

"Excuse me!" Ross hollered from the treeline as he approached, fuming. "Are you out of your *mind*? What is there to *discuss*? They're *predators*! They belong on the *mountain*. If they live among us, we will never be able to sleep with our eyes closed *again*!"

"Then, we will decide that fate together."

Ross ran off in a huff, cursing beneath his breath.

Ryan bugled loudly for the others to gather, his voice reaching out through the soft patter of steady rain to every corner of the Great Timbers.

***

"With Big Bob gone, *Ryan* should rightfully be his successor." The aging sow muttered to the group. "But that means it would be *his* responsibility to *protect* us, and I don't think the little man is up to the task! Big Bob would be disappointed if he knew--" She was interrupted by the bellow and squealing whistle of a small elk's bugle.

"Enough! Please!" Ryan grunted. "This has been a trying day for all of us. We need to keep a level *head* about things."

The word *head* made Ross wince. Nausea washed through his furry belly.

Ryan walked to the center of the circle of animals. A sea of black eyes was on him, each glistening in the bold array of colors fanning out across the gloomy evening sunset.

"As you all know, my *father...*" he stepped toward the raccoon, the fur around his eyes damp and matted from crying, "was a creature of *great* compassion."

A low rumble of voices sounded from the herd in agreement.

"With all the bounty that we have to offer here, you know as well as I do, he wouldn't have turned these cubs away to suffer, to *die* out there on the mountain, no matter *how* dangerous they are. He would have taken Kilgore *herself* in if she'd have asked with kindness."

Mixed opinions rumbled among the gathering.

"We must keep that same compassionate spirit. We mustn't turn our backs on other animals when there is a far more nefarious threat out there."

His eyes drifted to the spot where the hunters desecrated his idol. A spot where the cubs' mother also received her fate.

He turned to Arnold and Wesley and paused for a moment before speaking.

"If we let you live among us in the Great Timbers, would you agree to live by our rules and never harm *any* of us?"

A weasel and a badger waited with bated breath. Richard rose above them on his hind legs from the forest floor.

The bears thought for a moment. Finally, Arnold spoke up. "Yes, but... how will we survive?"

"The squirrels and opossums will train you to gather berries. The raccoons will point you to all the hives of bees for honeycomb. And Richard will lead you upstream to a fishing hole filled with trout. You can have your fill of those. But you mustn't harm a single creature in this meadow. Not *ever*. If we let you stay, you must learn to live as one of us in *peace*. You must swear before all of us here tonight that you two will not turn on us and that, if the time ever comes, you'll help us seek revenge for the loved ones we lost today."

"We swear," the cubs said in unison.

The birds chirped quietly to the deer while the squirrels and badgers further discussed the bizarre situation.

"Good. Will someone collect some berries and nuts for them tonight?"

"Aye, we shall," said a dusty, white opossum in the front, nodding his head on his thick neck, tufted in two-toned fur.

"Thank you." Ryan nodded respectfully. "Tomorrow, Ross, you and Richard should take them upstream and teach them how to fish. Let them get their bellies nice and full before the upcoming freeze."

"*Me*? Why *me*?" Ross asked.

"Because, my friend, I'm putting you in charge of watching them until we can trust them completely. After what you did yesterday with Kilgore, I have a lot of faith in you. Clearly, you're not one to shy away from a threat."

***

Night fell on the Great Timbers. The animals bedded down in the damp leaves and grass and tried their best to forget the day's events.

As the cold, northern winds gripped their icy fingers around them, Ryan sat awake in the meadow, looking at the stars above, seeking the peculiar antler-like cluster his father once called *the Alignment*.

He saw nothing but blurred dots as his black eyes once again filled with tears.

Thoughts of vengeance filled his mind, as did the haunting bleats and mews of his father before he took his final breaths.

He wished now, more than anything, that he could be a carefree child again, one without the responsibility of the herd resting hard on his laughable little spikes.

He craved that legendary alignment of the stars. If it were hovering above him, he'd have wished his father was beside him again.

To keep him warm. To offer wisdom about the potentially dangerous new cubs. And, more than anything, to guide them *all* through the years and tribulations ahead.

PART II:

The Return

26

The morning sun began its heavenly ascent, signaling the dawn of a late-autumn day in the Great Timbers. Creatures scurried about, trying to gather food for the morning's breakfast.

Two years had passed since the humans had taken Big Bob and Kilgore from this world.

In the years following the tragedy, Ryan took over training of the herds with his best friend, Edward, to help with the growing population. Their bond had only strengthened in the years since.

Over time, they'd both grown large and strong. Ryan was now the spitting image of his father.

With strengthened resolve, Ryan devoted himself to ending the senseless actions of any human who *dared* to enter the Great Timbers.

On this day, as the sun rose high in the sky, Ryan called the other elk, antelope, deer, and the new moose into the meadow for their daily exercises, just like Big Bob used to do. Ryan hadn't known it then, but the training that his father had been bestowing upon them was vital.

Ryan wasn't the only animal to change over the years.

Ross had become quite the soldier, promoted to one of Ryan's right-hand men and encouraged to train his own group of tree creatures in the art of nut-chucking.

Every day, Ross would gather his small but formidable army of squirrels, badgers, opossums, and raccoons to practice gathering and throwing nuts and rocks at targets from various heights and positions.

Today, they had an effigy of a human made of branches and leaves, tied with braided bark cordage by Ross's little hands.

They all practiced attacking it as though it were the real being destined to destroy them.

Ross stood on a branch overlooking the younger kits, masked eyes scanning the meadow, constantly alert and ready for the real threat to return.

Wesley and Arnold had grown into large grizzlies by now, both of them almost a mirror image of Kilgore, which Ryan found difficult to swallow some days, though he kept it inside.

Since that fateful day, the cubs had obeyed the laws set forth by the animals. They had since become steadily contributing members of their society, often returning from their trips upstream with salmon and trout to share with the other carnivores and omnivores.

They also became adept at scaling trees for hives, bringing back delicious honeycomb to share with their brethren.

Despite their size, they'd become loving, caring animals, thanks to the acceptance of the others in their time of need. No longer were they scrawny and emaciated. Now their stomachs were large and full, their fur lustrous.

When the other animals first took in Arnold and Wesley, there was some doubt as to whether they could be taught to live in harmony with the group. Though they may have been tempted to resort back to their mother's predatory ways, the temptation was never enough for them to jeopardize the acceptance, safety, and love of their newfound family.

Many of the animals had since found romance as well. Edward had his heart set on Kenna, a fawn who had grown to be a healthy, starry-eyed doe, though he hadn't found the nerve to tell her how he felt.

Ross swooned secretly over Heather from afar, never admitting it aloud for fear that she would just laugh. *A raccoon and a squirrel?* It seemed like a preposterous union. Still, he could not keep his eyes off her, adoring the nurturing, cinnamon-colored rodent in secret.

And Ryan found Star, an elk cow who had joined their herd during the most recent springtime, migrating to the Great Timbers with her family.

She stood at the edge of the tree line, waiting for Ryan to finish the daily training with the calves and yearlings. As Ryan approached, he was reminded how lucky he was to have her as his mate. Every day, he found himself more enamored with her than the last.

They gathered on top of the gently sloping convex hill, which, upon Big Bob's demise, changed the landscape of the meadow and the lives of those *in* it forever.

Ryan rubbed his nose against Star's ears, content in the moment with her.

Together, they watched as proud parents came to gather their young from the training circle. It seemed like every day, a newborn creature was brought into existence in the serenity of their idyllic piece of the world.

The young were regularly brought to the meadow, to the mound that served as Big Bob's grave, to meet their new age-appropriate playmates.

Proud mothers and fathers shared stories of the days when Ryan's father ruled the Great Timbers.

Despite the passage of time, the lack of his presence was still felt heavily by those who knew him. His demise had left a hole in the community that only time could slowly heal.

Though the years had come and gone, they had never forgotten about the events that devastated them all. Nor had they forgotten about the humans that caused it, though none had returned to their neck of the woods.

They all feared that sooner or later, that would change.

They knew they must be fully prepared to deal with the humans when the time was right. They vowed that lives would no longer be needlessly taken for sport.

Not without a fight.

Although there hadn't been any sign of the humans for several summers, they all knew in their hearts that the humans would someday return.

27

Still catching his breath after a brisk morning run, Ryan approached his raccoon pal, one who, in the years since Big Bob's passing, had become one of his best friends and closest confidantes.

"Morning, Ross. What're you up to today?"

"Shhhhhh!" The raccoon held a finger to his black lips from his favorite bough of the birch at the edge of the clearing.

Ryan followed the raccoon's masked eyes to the re-stuffed effigy.

The tiny critter stared at it with a scowl. Suddenly, he screamed, "Right flank, *attack*!"

Before Ryan knew what was happening, ten squirrels and two opossums jumped out onto the edges of their high-up branches in various trees to the right of the straw-stuffed human figures.

Each hurled nuts and rocks at it. A rain of small, solid objects battered the large doll, pelting it like a vicious hailstorm.

"Left flank, *attack*!"

This time, eight raccoons and three more opossums performed the same choreographed motions on the left.

One of the rocks knocked the effigy's head off. It rolled on the ground with a quiet *swish,* and the animals on both sides erupted in cheers and celebration.

Ross smiled contently at the devastated remains.

Ryan looked at the pile of busted sticks, straw, and pine cones that once stood roughly six feet tall.

"*Very* impressive."

"Line up in formation, warriors!" Ross barked the command, and his fighters scurried through the woods and meadow until they were all in a straight row before him. Ross walked down the line, looking for flaws with the furry warriors.

Suddenly, the raccoon burst into a fit of laughter. There, at the end of the line, stood a young, whitetail fawn aligned with the tree creatures. "I think you're lost, kid. The elk and deer meet over by the bend in the stream. Just go straight, then turn right. Second birch on your left. Can't miss it."

"No. I'm not lost." The fawn stepped forward bravely. "I want to fight with *you.* Everyone knows this is where *serious* fighters go. Rumor has it you've been training the treetop guardians for *years*." He stared for a moment and then flexed his tiny jaw in a serious manner. "I want to offer my services."

"Services? What services? You have nothing *for* me, kid. You don't even have *hands*. No thumbs at all! You can't clutch anything." Ross snarled as he bent down and picked up a fist-sized rock from the ground. "Can you throw this?"

"No. But watch this." The young fawn shook in place as if wicking away water. "Throw that rock in the air, just behind me."

Ross just stared at him.

"*Please.*"

Ross sighed heavily, tossed the rock into the air, and watched as the fawn kicked his hind leg with all of his might, connecting his hoof with the rock. With a resounding crunch, the rock jetted straight out and smacked a tree so violently that a shattered hunk of bark flew off.

"My aim is true, and I've been working on my kick for weeks."

Ross's eyes bulged with amazement, but he stayed composed. "What's your name, kid?"

"Friends call me Herbie."

"Well, Herbie, I think I can work with that. Welcome to the team." He held his tiny hand out to shake and then realized Herbie couldn't return it.

He awkwardly put his hand away and looked around at his army of squirrels, opossums, and raccoons, pleased.

"Good work, everyone! *Tomorrow*." He looked at Herbie, nodded, and then looked on toward the others. "Same time. Same place. *Dismissed*."

With a nod, the creatures dispersed.

Ryan noticed that even though the others had gone about their day, Ross sat in the low bough, staring off into the distance at the permanent mound where the grass grew greener and richer than the rest of the meadow. *The ground where their once-fearless leader had been laid to rest.*

Ryan watched him, recognizing the same listless, faraway stare that he, too, still got occasionally.

"I should have done something," Ross said, unblinking. "I should've *thrown* something. I should have thrown *myself* onto that human. They needed *him* more than they could ever need *me*," Ross said, teary-eyed. "I let him down, Ryan."

All this time later, the loss still burned in his heart.

"No, Ross. You didn't." Ryan felt a sense of camaraderie in that moment, having felt similarly.

Wishing he'd done more both with Kilgore *and* with the humans.

"I blame myself. I hope I never make that error again."

The elk was touched by the raccoon's words. "I appreciate your sense of loyalty, Ross, both to my father and to all of us. You did your best. He'd be so proud if he could see you right now."

"They'll be *back*, you know," Ross said, eyes shifting to the flat ridge on the mountain.

"I know." The solemn words fell like hefty rocks from the bull's mouth.

Ross's eyes drifted over to Ryan. "Someday, we'll have the chance to show *them* what it's like to be hunted."

28

Fierce and graceful, Edgar swooped down one blustery day upon the northern winds, hoping to capture a groundhog or rabbit for dinner. Though starving and weak, Edgar, a bald eagle, circled over the meadow in search of some easy prey.

Soon, he spotted a rabbit. Edgar lowered his head and dive-bombed toward it. Just as he thought the bunny was locked in his sight, his landing spot blurred, and he crashed right into a mound of dirt, severely misjudging its distance.

Ryan watched the scene, concerned.

Edgar sat up, shook his head, and looked around, trying to focus in on the elusive rabbit.

He saw a blur dead ahead. Ravenous, he stood, flapped his enormous wings, and chased it.

The jackrabbit stood frozen as the great bald eagle flew right past him as though he didn't exist and slammed beak-first into a pine tree at the edge of the woods.

He lay there on the ground, head pounding.

Ryan trotted over to the eagle. "Excuse me, what do you think you're *doing*?"

"Trying to find food! Do you mind?" With one strong flap, Edgar spread his wings and arose from the ground and cruised back into the sky.

"*Yes*, I mind," the elk squealed into the air.

No sooner did the words leave his mouth that the eagle clambered to his talons, sprinted, and crash-landed again, tumbling through the dry dirt. Swallowing his wounded pride, the eagle dusted himself off, still discombobulated from the hit.

"I thought your kind had keen eyesight?" Ryan asked with a hint of sarcasm.

Edgar stopped dusting himself off and squinted his eyes to better focus on the elk.

Suddenly, the eagle jumped backward, scrambling. "Ahhhh! Please don't eat me! I'm sorry! I wouldn't have talked to a bear like that knowingly. I meant *no* disrespect."

Ryan laughed. "You really *are* blind, aren't you?" He cleared his throat, trying to stifle his giggling. "I'm Ryan. I'm an elk, not a bear."

Edgar squinted and backed up. With every backward step, he could see the bull a little clearer.

Ryan stared, watching how hard the bird had to squint to see him. "Sorry, Roger. I can see things well as long as they're far away, but when I get close…" The bird shrugged.

"My name is Ryan, *not Roger*."

"Sorry," Edgar chuckled nervously. "I tend to forget things because of all the hard falls."

Ryan didn't respond. He simply eyed the bird, fascinated by the creature's surprising wing span and strange, taloned feet. Rarely had the owl ever gotten close enough to examine, always staying up in the trees. Hence, the elk found this new specimen especially curious.

He lowered his head in frustrated defeat. "Randall, I'm sorry I'm so scattered with my thoughts."

Ryan opened his mouth to correct him but thought better of it.

"It's just that… I haven't eaten in so long. I can't seem to catch anything! On top of it, I get lost every time I fly around. I forget where I am. Ever since I was born, my eyesight has been terrible. My family always hunted for me. But now they're gone." Edgar's tone grew serious. "And now I'm alone, trying my best to feed myself. But it seems… *impossible*."

"Maybe you could join us. You'd have to adhere to the same rules as our grizzlies. But I'm sure Arnold and Wesley will share fish with you.

During the warmer months, we always have an abundance." Ryan offered with great empathy.

***

Ryan stared out at the circle of beady eyes before him. "Now, I know it's an odd request, but look at what a large part of our society Wes and Arnie have become since we took them in."

"I don't have a problem sharing some trout with him. The rainbows have just spawned, and there's plenty to go around." Wesley said, resting his paw full of long claws on his knee. He adjusted himself on the tree trunk he was seated on.

"Yeah, I suppose I don't have a problem with it. I mean, Wes and I know what it's like to lose your family."

"And what it's like to starve." Wesley nodded.

"I just don't see what good it does to take in someone who brings no skills with him," Ross objected.

But Edgar's mind was too many miles away to be offended. His neck sat at a 90-degree angle, eyes staring far off into the field at the crystal-clear effigy in his line of sight. He chuckled. "You guys build that thing?" He lifted a wing to point off in the distance.

"Yeah." Ross crossed his arms and tried to hide the annoyed expression from his face. "Why?"

"It's a good likeness."

That caught Ryan's attention. "What do you mean?"

"I mean, it looks just like a human from here. You nailed the shape."

"Wait," Ryan trotted in place, eyes locked on the bird, "you mean, you've *seen* one?"

"Oh, my, *no*." He laughed.

Ryan didn't move.

"No, no. I've seen a *lot* of them."

A badger gasped.

Ross's eyes grew large.

Edgar turned back to the group, squinting hard to try to focus on their blurred faces. "Yeah, they've been building that wooden peak for a long time, making all kinds of racket."

"*Where*?" Ross stepped forward.

The eagle outstretched his wing again, just to the right of the rocky plateau that formed a ledge in the middle of the mountain. "Couple miles back that way, at the end of the road."

"What's a *road*?" A jackrabbit asked, confused.

Edgar seemed nonchalant. "It's one of those paths the wheeled things ride on."

"What's a *wheeled thing*?" A sow asked, stamping her hooves in place anxiously.

The bald eagle giggled. "Wow, you all don't get out much, *do you*? I'll bet there's a whole *world* of stuff you don't know about."

"This wooden peak, can you take us there? Can you show us?" Ross asked, stepping closer, nearly in the middle of the circle now.

"Sure!" Edgar doubled over with laughter. "For a trout, I'll take you to the world's end right now. Not that I've found that, I assure you." Edgar held out a wing to comfort them. "But, yes, I'll lead you to wherever you want to go."

Ryan looked around.

"Well? What do you all think?"

"I think," Ross looked up at the bull with sincerity, "we'd be *fools* to turn down a pair of eyes in the sky."

"Aye." Richard, the beaver, agreed with a nod. "It would be wise to finally have a good lookout in our employ." His eyes drifted to the treetops full of squirrel spotters, all lounging lazily across Watchman's Line, just as they had the day Kilgore entered their lives.

"Well, then," Ryan strode toward the eagle and smiled, though the bird could not see it. "Welcome to the Great Timbers."

29

Despite the brand-new construction and the thick, insulated walls, cold air still seemed to penetrate the lodge that Jimmy had built on the other side of the mountain range, several miles away from the meadow.

Building the Elk Mountain Lodge had taken two years and 4.2 million dollars. *Still, Jimmy* had total faith that it would attract the highest-paying hunters. His accountants and financial advisors were convinced he would make their money back. The shocking prices he planned to charge to elite hunters worldwide would have Jimmy and his moneymen back in the black in no time.

And the first four takers had just arrived.

The triangular lodge was an architectural marvel equipped with all of the conveniences a modern-day hunter could ask for. Inspired by the *Triangle Cliff House* created by Matthias Arndt in Germany and the *Lima Cabin* in Chevlav Mountain, Iran, it featured a fairly steeply graded A-frame roof that went from its apex straight into the ground on the sides. It boasted a wall of windows spanning the entire back and front-facing sides of the building, providing its inhabitants with a jaw-dropping panorama of the woods from the back and a breathtaking view of the fully-stocked lake whose shore was a thirty-foot jaunt from the front door.

The *Elk Mountain Lodge* had a vaulted ceiling, wooden-rail outer balconies on the first and second floors, and a large fireplace in a foyer loaded to the absolute *brim* with taxidermied animal mounts forming a stunning menagerie of kills, all frozen in various poses.

The elegant pyramid was nestled into a deep plot of dirt road property just a few short miles from the scenic overlook at Fremont Canyon.

All materials had to be hauled onto the property in small batches. The road was narrow for commercial-grade equipment. Jimmy paid the construction workers handsomely and had each sign Non-Disclosure Agreements to ensure that the lodge's location stayed shrouded in secrecy.

With seclusion and secrecy in mind, Jimmy even went as far as to hire a luxury shuttle driver, who worked for the lodge full-time, to take clients from a specified location in the nearby town of Casper to the property in a vehicle with blacked-out windows. This ensured that guests could not return on their own and hunt without using Jimmy's services. In the massive territory of unsullied land that Wyoming offered, obscurity remained an easy task.

Jimmy didn't trust anyone except Notches when it came to keeping the location of the lodge quiet. Not just so that they could keep the news of their little trophy-filled oasis from local sportsmen but to prevent anyone from finding out what really happened to Mickey.

Deemed a simple disappearance from shrugging local law enforcement deputies who, years back, found his single-wide trailer empty with his immaculate white Chevy parked in the driveway, Jimmy often stressed about what would happen if the old man's body was found, or worse, somehow traced back to *them*.

Would the jury buy their story if a coyote abandoned his skull on the side of the highway?

Would Notches lie about Jimmy's involvement for some kind of plea deal? He saw it all the time in his former line of work. Sometimes, Jimmy himself even *facilitated* those sorts of *quid pro quo* deals.

And *then* there was a part of him…

A part that always wondered if Notches had actually been involved in the man's demise somehow. He always shook it off, telling himself that Notches had been with him, preoccupied with his poached kills.

But Notches's lack of sympathy for his co-worker always struck him as odd.

Worst case scenario, Nicholas had gotten vigilante retribution for Mickey trying to kill his pricey mutt.

Best case scenario, the man was just a demented *sociopath* with no feelings.

Either way, Notches had since been promoted to Jimmy's go-to for all things land-related in Mickey's stead. In the years since Mickey died, Jimmy thought it wise to keep his friends close…

And his enemies even *closer*.

30

Jimmy bent down by the large fireplace in the foyer, fueling the flames with wood he'd paid his nephew to spend a week chopping, which all now sat in a neat, shoulder-height stack along one side of the first-story wrap-around porch. The intoxicating smell of smoky pine filled the open floor plan. Flames crackled quietly in the hearth.

He stood and glanced around.

The building astounded him.

Every choice in the design was made with care, all coming together into a cohesive work of art. A smile stretched across his face as he examined the centerpiece hanging on the wall above the fireplace to greet all who entered: the plaque-mounted head of the elk Notches had shot from the ridge.

Nearby, Notches sat at a glass dinner table, rubbing linseed oil on the gouged stock of his rifle. He listened intently to the conversation of their first paying guests as they settled into their respective sleeping areas along the upstairs inner balcony.

Listening to the men talk bothered him enormously. Just because they were rich enough to pay the twenty-five-thousand-per-person fee Jimmy charged for lodging, food, tags, and guided tour to the area's hot spots didn't mean these men were *hunters*.

To Notches, they were just rich, spoiled frat boys. Weekend warriors who had nothing better to do than shell out trust-fund money for the luxury of having outfitters practically aim the gun *for* them. They were just egocentric millionaires, like *Jimmy*, bored of their local spots and too lazy to scour for something better on their own.

Jimmy patted one of the young men on the back, taking him in his arm like an old friend. "Come on over! Now that you're settled, come have a drink."

They sat together at the table with Notches. He glanced up at them, mouth pursed, skin like a sun-weathered old cowboy who'd spent too many years on a sun-scorched range.

"Tell us a little about yourselves." Jimmy raised an ornate crystal bottle of bourbon from the center of the table, pouring each drink into a matching, etched glass.

"Tom York." The heavyset man offered a little wave as his friends piled into the empty chairs beside him.

"Charles Bright," the next man said, pulling his chair in. "Everyone calls me Chuck." Jimmy slid a glass of booze over to him, and Chuck held up his hand, gently waving it away. "Nah, I'm all set."

"Yeah, this lame-wad doesn't partake in any of the fun stuff," another said. He pointed to himself with a thumb and flashed a blinding smile full of bleached teeth. "I'm Mike Hanson, by the way."

"Stan Collins," said the man who sat next to Jimmy. He sighed and swiped the brand-new hunter-orange beanie off his head and onto the table, revealing a short frock of messy red hair beneath. "But you guys can call me The Master."

The clients all laughed aloud. Mike slammed his hand on the glass table, rattling all the glasses on it. "Oh my God, bro. *What*? The *Master*?" He giggled at a decibel far too loud for their proximity.

Stan grinned and snapped back playfully, "Shut up, *Michael*."

Just then, Stan noticed the price tag was still on his beanie. He slid it beneath the table hoping no one would see him remove it.

But Notches saw. He pinched his eyes closed and breathed deep through his nose before returning to his maintenance ritual.

"So, how do you boys know each other," Jimmy asked, raising his dirty-blond eyebrows.

Notches side-eyed him.

"We met in school," Mike grinned and lifted the drink to his lips, wincing with the sip.

"Let me guess. I take you for *Ivy League* boys." Jimmy smiled. "*Amiright*?"

Mike nodded, arms crossed in front of his barrel chest.

"Not Harvard..." Jimmy rubbed his chin and then smacked the table, wiping his fingerprint smudges immediately without thinking. "*Yale*. Final answer."

"*Holy*--" Thomas said, face twisted in shock. "How did you...?"

After a moment, Notches growled. "It's written on his *shirt, genius*."

Jimmy flashed Notches an irritated glare, brown eyes piercing. Notches wasn't bothered by it in the slightest.

The young men looked around and saw that Mike's jacket was unzipped just enough to see a piece of the giant, navy "A" and "L" on the heathered gray backdrop.

"*Touche*!" Tom burst into a cackle as if it were the funniest thing he'd heard in a month.

"New Haven. Alriiiight. Nice area up there, New England." Jimmy leaned over to stroke Keeka's head as she sat patiently nearby, quietly watching the exchange.

"Yeah, but the hunting *there* is," Tom made a sour face, "*blah*. Plus this *view*." He motioned out the panoramic set of windows at the sunset-kissed lake beyond. "This is like a little piece of *Heaven* up here."

"Yeah, this place is amazing." Mike eyed the taxidermied heads on the wall. His eyes fixed on the adult grizzly, standing on her hind legs, frozen in mid-swipe, roaring for eternity.

"Glad you think so." Jimmy smiled with satisfaction and crossed his arms. "You're our lucky *firsts*."

"Oooh, maiden voyage, eh?" Mike said, taking a swig of bourbon and exhaling loudly. "*Wow. That*'ll put hair on your chest!" He popped the glass hard against the fragile table, and Jimmy stared at it, trying to force a genuine-looking smile.

"As you *are* our first clients at the *Elk Mountain Lodge*, we want you to know we are *always* open to suggestions. Let us know anything we can do to make your stay as comfortable and exciting as possible. We want to make this a paradise you all want to return to. The little slice of Eden that you tell all your friends about."

31

Ross, Wesley, and Arnold decided they did not want to wait another moment to investigate Edgar's allegations of human activity. If they were in danger, Ross wanted them to know about it immediately so they could prepare and protect their loved ones.

Wesley and Arnold insisted on joining. Partially to protect the raccoon and partially because they wanted to see for themselves.

Edgar soared majestically in the air above them, pointing out the easiest path to the triangle, squawking regularly to illustrate which way they should go.

The miles had been arduous on their feet and joints, none used to travelling such great distances with any regularity.

After all, the bountiful Great Timbers provided everything they ever wanted.

***

In the Timbers, Edward peered through the darkness and examined the settling herd until he saw Kenna. The bashful buck approached her quietly so he didn't disturb Star from her slumbers. Ryan's mate hadn't been feeling well the last few days, and the other harem members were tending to her. Being the nurturing doe she was, Kenna hadn't left Star's side in two days.

Edward approached, fearful of being tongue-tied or clumsy in his approach. "Kenna," he whispered, "would you like to go with me for a walk?"

He lowered his head to wait for the answer, too shy to look the beauty in the eyes. He knew if she said yes, he'd have miles to finally tell her how he felt about her.

She stood, carefully walked around the sleeping does, rubbed her nose on his ear, and smiled.

"I'd love to."

***

Just beyond the treeline, Ross saw the triangle Edgar spoke of. His heart sank as he watched smoke billow out of the hole in the top. It was true.

Humans *had*, in fact, returned.

Or, *for all he knew,* they'd maybe never left.

"I'm going to have a look around the back," Wesley whispered, walking off into the woods.

"Be *careful*," Arnold whispered back as he and Ross approached the front porch with trepidation.

Ross and Arnold examined the structure's interior by peering in the glass from behind a large Bird of Paradise plant. Quietly, Ross climbed on Arnold's back so he could see better.

Ross recognized Notches's leathery face right away. In the years since, he hadn't been able to shake the traumatic images that he'd seen from the tree that day.

The *beheading…*

"We should go back and tell the others," he whispered, his black eyes never straying from the man who defiled their beloved king.

Arnold looked toward the fireplace, and tears flooded his eyes. He placed a hand over his mouth and leaned against the wall to stop himself from falling over in a moment of weakness.

It was his mother.

Standing on her hind legs.

Frozen in a vicious pose with firelight dancing in her eerie, glass eyes.

Arnold wanted to collapse. His heart broke seeing her like that. Like some toy for amusement in some forever-unnatural state.

Beside her, Big Bob's mounted head hung on the wall.

"Ross, look away," Arnold whispered.

Ross just stood there, trembling. Too horrified to move.

Arnold searched for the words to comfort Ross, but he'd never been good about finding the right things to say. Soft, comforting sentiments were hard for a grizzly to muster.

Ross grabbed Arnold's neck, squeezing as he cried. Tears wicked off Ross's black mask onto Arnold's shoulder. But, now, Arnold was sobbing, too. They shed tears together in dusk's dim, indigo light as the trees disappeared into the approaching darkness.

***

Keeka's ears perked up at the quiet rustling outside. Her master and his friends didn't seem to hear it, but it was too loud for her to ignore. She stood up to investigate, not drawing the attention of any of the humans. As a dog, she had come accustomed to being overlooked and *underestimated.*

As she approached the front door, she saw a grizzly and a raccoon just outside the front porch railing.

She let out a high-pitched whine and clawed gently at the back of the door.

Almost as if it were an automatic motion, one he'd done a thousand times before during the months of construction, Jimmy rose from the table and opened the front door to let her out, never looking at her once.

She shot outside, and he closed the door, immediately returning to the table where he laughed and talked with the other humans.

Once outside, Keeka raced down the porch steps and stood a healthy distance away. "What are you *doing here?!*"

The animals turned to face her, startled, ready to scurry.

"*Keeka*?" Ross narrowed his eyes, unsure if it was her.

She stared at him, too, unsure where exactly she knew him from but vaguely recognizing him. "Who are you?" She peered through the darkness at the moving shapes, taking in the raccoon's familiar scent in big whiffs. "How did you know my name?"

"You..." Arnold lowered the raccoon to the ground, and Ross cautiously approached the wolfdog in the shadowed area below the porch.

"It's me. We met a few years back in the meadow. You came to warn us. You said your name was Keeka."

He pressed his tiny hands together and then fanned them back out submissively. "We mean you no harm, I promise. Not you, at least. My name is Ross. This is Arnold. His brother Wesley's around back. Our friend," He pointed up at the bald eagle standing atop the white side-by-side, almost blending into each other with their similar colors, "told us about this place. We had to come see for ourselves."

"You have to go," she blurted frantically. "If my master or his friends see you, they'll kill you. You'll end up in there."

As she whipped her head toward the house, she caught sight of the elk's head on the wall and remembered it all so clearly. Despite the long passage of time that felt like decades to her, it all came rushing back…

That day in the meadow…

"Our mother," Arnold started pointing at Kilgore inside, high on her hind legs looking like she was ready to pounce on her prey, "is she--"

Keeka somberly looked at the ground. "All of those animals in there may look like it, but they aren't alive. It's some kind of sick ornament they make for a house."

"What is a house?" Ross asked, taking another slow step toward her.

"It's the thing we live in. Usually, mine's a box, but then my master's friend made… *this*." She looked at the triangular building like it was some monstrosity.

"What's a… *master*?" Arnold sounded innocent and docile for such a giant creature.

"It's the human that owns me," Keeka said, cocking a furry brow as if it were common knowledge.

Arnold and Ross looked at each other for a moment with confusion.

"You all have to go. Quick, before they see you. Before you end up like--" Her words trailed off as her moonlit-blue eyes settled on the macabre menagerie adorning the walls inside.

"Why are they here?" Ross asked, staring in at the humans.

"They find *joy* in killing. All my life, there have been so many dead things… *staring at me*." The thought raised her hackles, and she shook her whole body as if shaking off water just to cleanse her thoughts of the notion.

Keeka stared at them, a fierce look in her wild eyes. "You should go. I don't want to see either of you up there next. Get your brother and leave before it's too late."

***

Still blathering on about a fishing trip he'd had in Massachusetts as a boy, Jimmy mindlessly opened the door to let the dog in. She usually did her business quickly, and, like always, there she was, waiting obediently on the porch, long tail brushing the fallen leaves from the deck with a quiet swish.

"--I mean, we were stuck in that cabin for *days* from the storm." He motioned for her to come inside with his head, and she did without a noise.

Just as Jimmy shut the door, he glanced through the wide glass wall beside it and saw something move through the darkness.

Something too big to be human.

Forehead wrinkled with concern, he walked over to the massive window and cupped his hands, pressing his face to the recently cleaned glass.

Notches perked up a little in his chair, noticing the abrupt stop to one of Jimmy's overly long tales with no satisfying payoff.

His eyes settled on the row of pines at the edge of the lake, just beyond the porch, catching a glimpse of something that made him step back fearfully.

The moonlit shape of a stout, full-grown bear. Jimmy touched his chest, feeling his heart pound beneath his thick sweatshirt. "Notches! Come here."

Notches joined him at the window, Winchester Magnum in hand. He stared out through the glass.

Nothing.

"What am I looking at?"

"There was a *bear*." Jimmy grinned.

"You *drunk*?" Notches snickered.

"Hardly." He stood on his toes, trying to get a better view. "Ballsy of him to come so close to the lodge like that."

Notches smiled back at the men seated around the table. "Well, boys, if that's true, looks like the big game is already comin' to *you*."

32

Edward walked next to Kenna, unsure how to tell her about his feelings for her. The mere presence of her walking next to him, alone, made the fur on his back dance anxiously.

What if she laughed?

What if she cared for another?

What if she told the other does, and he became the joke of the meadow--

"Edward?" Her voice, sweet as honey, interrupted his barrage of nervous thoughts. "Are you alright? You seem… distant." She lowered her head to briefly graze.

"Well, there's something I have to tell you. Wh--" His voice came out as a squeak. He cleared his throat and tried again, "Wh-what, with the *humans* about, I didn't want to wait another day without telling you. I don't know how you feel about me, but," he hesitated. "I like you." He let out a nervous laugh. "Kind of a lot."

She lifted her head and smiled, cheeks hot with a bashful blush.

"It's just that you're so kind, not just to me, but to *all* of us. You take care of everyone. Just like how you've been helping Star the last few days."

"Poor thing," she said quietly. "She's been so ill lately. We aren't sure what's wrong with her. If something happened to her," she paused, and her sparkling eyes met his again, "Ryan would be devastated."

"I hope she's alright."

"Me too."

"But that's what I mean. You're so good with everyone. Anyone would be lucky to have you. I've seen you with the little ones, too. I think you'd be an amazing mother."

The words made her face grow serious. "That's what I want, too. To bring new life to the meadow. Something that will live on long after I do."

"I want that, too." He smiled. "I've always admired you from afar, hoping you'd notice me."

"Oh, I've *noticed* you alright." She giggled. "You're the best-looking buck in the Great Timbers. How could I *not* notice you?"

They were both quiet for a moment, just staring into each other's eyes. Edward took a step closer, and she leaned over and nuzzled him.

"Can we… stay here tonight?" Kenna looked out from the unobstructed slope at the incredible view of the night sky. "The stars look so lovely from up here."

"I'd like that," Edward said, his chest swelling with joy. They walked beside one another, closer than before. The air between them felt electric.

A few feet away, Edward bent his legs and buckled to a patch of soft grass beneath a nearby tree.

Kenna joined him in the leaf litter. She laid her head on the solid buck's back and closed her eyes. Their tails gently fluttered with joy.

"I don't want this night to end," she cooed, staring at the constellations above with heavy eyelids.

Edward smiled, content. "Neither do I."

33

"So, what's the plan for the morning?" Tom hollered from the upstairs balcony, seated on the corner of his queen-sized bed. He removed his glasses and wiped the lenses with the bottom of his shirt before putting them back on his face.

"Well, we'll get your butts outta bed at 04:00 hours. Get some gourmet coffee in ya'. Get you suited up, and then get you out on that trail for the adventure of your *life*." Jimmy flashed his best salesman smile as he filled a small cooler full of IPAs and a diet soda for Charles.

Stan chuckled a little. "We're already here, man. You don't have to keep sellin' us on it."

"Oh, shut up." Mike threw a creme-colored pillow at him from the balcony. "You're such a wet blanket, you stooge. If the guy wants to give us a little pep-talk, let him do it."

"I'm just sayin' he's over here talking about seein' bears and stuff, trying to get us psyched for the trip, but we're already excited, man."

"I *did* see a bear," Jimmy asserted.

Notches scoffed and looked down at the contents of his hunting pack splayed all over the brand-new woven rug beside the fireplace, double-checking that he had everything in order.

Jimmy smirked. "He's right. You boys should get some sleep. Got an early day tomorrow."

34

Arnold, Wesley, and Ross arrived back at the meadow in the darkness of the morning, long before the sun had thought to rise. Most of the animals were still sleeping, but Ryan was wide awake. He'd awaited their return, munching grass to calm his fraying nerves.

The news of the human's presence and the peril that his friends might be in gnawed at his soul.

And then there was *Star*, the love of his life, who had been weak and ill for days. It was hard to even get near her with the protective swarm of does and sows always trying to soothe her.

And where was *Edward* when he needed to talk? He hadn't seen his best friend since the afternoon prior.

As his friends approached, Ryan found at least some of his fears had subsided. They were safe, and that was *something*, at least.

"What's the news?"

"Well, it's not good. The humans… they're back. They've built some kind of triangular box near the lake on the other side of the mountain. We spoke to Keeka--"

"Wait, the--"

Ross interrupted, "The very same. I was just as shocked as you are. She called it a 'house.' She was trying to help us. Ryan, the triangle is big. There were more humans in it last night than the day that your dad," he stopped himself, changing the subject. "Arnold and I counted six of them."

"Six?!" Ryan nearly dropped the long strands of grass from his lips.

Ross was solemn.

It was clear there was more on his mind. He opened his mouth to speak, hesitated, and then closed it again, never taking his black eyes off the ground by the elk's feet.

"Ross, are you alright?"

Arnold chimed in, "He saw something that really upset him. Well, something that upset us all." His face grew long, and his nose scrunched to one side as he fought to stave off the sudden onset of tears.

"What? What did you see?" Ryan's eyes were the widest they'd ever seen him. He was soaking up every word.

Ross looked up at Ryan and itched the back of his head absentmindedly. "They have... Big Bob there."

Ryan was confused.

The statement made no sense.

"What do you mean they have him? My father is dead. You *watched* him die."

"Oh, I'm well aware," Ross said, voice shaky. "The humans they have his…"

Ross couldn't say the word.

Arnold cleared his throat. "His… *head*, Ryan. On the wall."

The words coming from the bear's mouth made the bull feel like he was being crushed by a boulder.

"They had our mother, too. I don't know how. She was going like this." Wesley posed in the position he'd seen the grizzly in, snarling expression and all. "But, she wasn't moving."

Arnold took another step forward. "She looked alive, but Keeka assured us she wasn't. It was just some sort of *illusion*. She said they only *look* alive." He looked up at the elk. "It's *morbid*, Ryan."

Wesley's voice got louder, nearly a roar. "They're treating our mother like a *decoration*!"

35

Kenna awoke to the indigo dawn and kissed Edward softly on the forehead.

Edward stirred when he felt her lips. Soon, his eyes opened, and he smiled. "I wish I could lay here forever with you," he murmured, struggling to stand and stretch, "but *Ryan*, you know how he worries…"

"Oh yes," she chuckled, knowing full well the bull was a bundle of nerves and stress.

Suddenly, Edward heard something that made him scramble.

They froze in place, listening intently.

When it happened again, Edward nearly skittered off the sheer drop-off, panicked.

It was the sound of leaves rustling underfoot.

"Do you hear that?"

Kenna stood, too, and pricked her ears.

The two were perfectly still.

Everything was quiet.

"Come on," Edward said, motioning with the swing of his head. "Let's get back to--"

BOOM!

Edward's words were cut short by the thunderous noise, shattering their idyllic world instantly.

The vaguely-familiar tone rattled the buck's nerves the moment it sounded.

"RUN!" He screamed at Kenna.

But she had already taken off, bounding like a scared jackrabbit into the treeline, tripping clumsily over her own legs, toppling awkwardly onto the sloping ground.

He raced after, watching in horror as she tumbled into gravel and pine needles, trying her best to scramble back onto her unwilling feet.

"Kenna," he bleated at the top of his lungs.

Kenna was in a frenzied daze, struggling to get away.

Fighting to stay on her feet.

Failing.

That's when he saw the stream of garnet fluid trailing back to her haunches, spattering the trail behind her as she sprung around.

"Woooooohooo!"

Edward turned again, heart beating. From a ridge line in the distance, he saw movement. They were silhouettes in the blue morning dawn, chilling specters that made Edward's heart nearly pound out of its cavity.

They were humans.

***

"Not the cleanest shot, but you got 'er," Stan said, massaging Tom's shoulder roughly with one hand as they traipsed down the steep mountain path.

"Yeah," Chuck snickered, "but he was *aimin'* for the *buck!*"

"You couldn't hit the broad side of a *barn*, Tom," Mike added at a decibel far too loud for the sport. "Think you need a new *prescription* for those *glasses*."

"Yeah, yeah. Yuck it up. I don't know what *you*'re having tonight, but *I'm* havin' venison," Tom mumbled quietly as they shuffled down the hill together.

"Well done," Notches said, impressed. He pulled a long-range walkie-talkie out of his pack and depressed the button. "Yo, Jimmy-Joe, I'm going to send you the coordinates for the big ol' doe *Tommy-Gun* here just dropped. Bring the side-by-side."

The hiss of static came through on the other end, followed by a, "Yep, copy that."

***

Edward was frozen in fear, unable to move.

Kenna's legs buckled hard at the knees. Her eyes were wide with shock. She tumbled through a thicket, tangling herself in the shrubbery, then collapsed to the ground in the clearing just beyond.

"*Kenna!*" Edward screamed.

BOOM!

Another bullet struck the tree just in front of him, missing his chest by mere inches.

The impact shot bark shrapnel into the air.

Frightened, he galloped off into the trees ahead.

***

"Here, want to borrow my *glasses*, Stan?" Mike cackled.

"See, this, this right here, this is why hunting is more of a *solitary* sport," Tom said, waving a hand at them. "You're all being way too loud right now."

Notches hunched next to the stilled doe. "Come on, Tom, get in 'ere for a picture."

Tom, smiling broadly, crouched beside the doe in his head-to-toe woodland camouflage. Notches took his glove off with his teeth, clenching the fingers of it in his tight jaw as he took a series of stills with his phone.

Afterward, he put his glove back on, wiped his runny, red nose, and grinned. "Congrats, kid. First person to make it on the website."

Tom nodded, eyes locked on his kill as he stroked her fur.

"Now you know what you gotta do, right?" Notches offered a mischievous look, eyes flashing in the morning dimness like a flash of green lightning. He poked her upper chest with his index finger a few times and grinned.

"It's *tradition.*"

36

Edgar overshot his landing spot by several feet and crashed into a tree branch. Heather and Ross turned to see the eagle brushing leaves off his feathers as he climbed onto the branch.

"Where's Ryan," he screeched.

"Over here, Edgar." Ryan shook his head, fighting the urge to roll his eyes at how ridiculous the bird was. "What? What is it? Did you find Edward? What about Kenna?"

Edgar's eyes grew large, chest heaving. He swallowed hard. "Edward's on his way back, but…"

He hesitated.

"But, what?" Ryan bleated impatiently.

Edgar ruffled his feathers and composed himself. "It's… *Kenna*."

***

By sunrise, all of the animals of the Great Timbers had heard the news and had arrived in the meadow to share their grief.

Wails of sorrow could be heard throughout the gathering.

Ryan walked over to the mound where Big Bob was buried. The others assembled in a circle around him with weakened Star at his side.

"The humans have returned. Kenna is *gone*. What they've done to my father and Kilgore," fury bubbled up beneath his fur, making his neck stretch and straighten, "is sickening. It's *unforgivable*. We *have* to fight back. We can not stand idly by and let these murderers take more lives, more family members!" His voice came out with renewed hatred, seething from his flattened, herbivorous teeth.

"They've placed my father's head on display. They've made a *plaything* out of Arnold and Wesley's mother. If we don't stop them, they will keep murdering us until every last one of us is gone! They must *pay* for these atrocities! We *must* defend our *home* and put an end to this. I, for one, will *not* be their prey! No one will blame you if you wish to leave, to find someplace safer. If you stay, you *fight*."

"But... there's nothing we can do," a glum marmot muttered.

"Yes, if we stay and fight, we're defenseless against their *boom-sticks*," a red fox yelled.

The tears of sorrow turned into sounds of anger and hatred.

The chatter among the animals grew.

As the discontent among the animals grew, Ross raised his hand to calm them. He stepped forward.

"We shouldn't be surprised. We all knew this day was coming. We've been training for this. Every pinecone and rock prepared us for today. They are coming. We will take those humans down if we stick together and work as a team. We are faster. We are smarter. And we know this land better than they *ever will*! When the time comes, we shall be ready for them!"

Ryan looked around at the animals as they stared at each other in nervous silence, most subtly nodding in agreement.

He couldn't help but wonder which of them might fall prey to the humans next.

PART III:

The Reckoning

37

There had been no sign of the humans by the time the darkness of night had arrived in the Great Timbers. Ryan and Star stood side-by-side out in the meadow. Ross's voice rang out through the crisp air, discussing strategies with his army of climbers, lookouts, and chuckers.

Star watched as Arnold and Wesley made their way up the dirt-worn path up the side of the mountain, their dark bodies barely visible in the darkness, like two writhing black shadows.

"Where are they headed?"

Ryan followed her line of sight until he saw them. He replied quietly, "I don't know."

His mind was a million miles away.

Not worried about the animals around him.

Instead, worried *for* them.

Finally, after a long silence, he spoke.

"After what happened to Kenna," Ryan stared off at the grass and snapped back into the moment, "you should hide tomorrow. Take cover somewhere safe at the far edge of the timbers, and I can send for you when this is over."

"But, Ryan," she protested weakly.

"I insist, Star. With you already feeling so ill, I wouldn't be able to live with myself if something happened to you." He spoke softly, eyes trained on the grass. "*Please?*"

"If you insist." She tensed her jaw. "I'll miss you."

"I'll miss you, too. Hopefully, it is not for long."

"Please be careful." She whispered, knowing that Ryan had already planned to do his best. She leaned against him and affectionately rubbed the side of her face along his long, brown mane.

He gazed at his beloved for a moment before his eyes drifted to the stars, brightening when he saw something he hadn't thought about in ages...

The Alignment.

It was an event he hadn't seen since he was a yearling, peering up at the brilliant sea of sparkles with his father in almost this very spot. The memory brought him joy, filling his heart with peace and nostalgia.

Though he couldn't have imagined it possible, he missed his father more than ever.

Star looked up at the sky as well and smiled weakly. "What are you looking at?"

"The *Alignment*," Ryan replied, as if in a trance. "My father always said that every now and then, the stars form the shape of elk antlers."

She looked at Ryan, watching his black eyes glimmer.

"He also said that if you *wish* upon the Alignment, it comes true."

She smiled. "Well, does it *work*?"

Ryan turned to her with glassy eyes full of tears.

Ones for his father.

Ones for Kenna.

Ones for his heartbroken best friend.

And ones for the animals that might be slain in the battle for their land.

For their *freedom*.

For their *lives*.

He took a deep breath and blinked, letting a stray tear roll down the curves of his majestic face. "We'll *see*."

38

Jimmy waltzed into the lodge from the cleaning station outside, holding a large slab of deer meat in his red-smeared hands. "Cheers to you, Tom. Tonight we *feast*!" He said the last word with a growl as if he would have beaten his chest with a balled fist had it not been full of freshly field-dressed venison.

"Yeah!" Stan cheered, holding a fist up in the air. "Way to go, Tommy-Gun!"

Jimmy dropped the slab of meat on a large cutting block in the kitchen area with a reverberating *thunk*. As he put his apron on, he looked at Notches and motioned his head, insisting the man join him. "Yo! You wanna bring in the rest so we can get it all prepped, vac-u-sealed, and in the ice box for these fellas?"

Mike noticed. He spoke up. "Hey, Jim, I can help you do that."

Jimmy put his hand out like a football player. "No, no, that's not necessary. We got this. It all comes included in the price." He chuckled even though there was no joke to be found. "You guys grab a beer, shower up, relax. You earned it today.

Notches and I'll get this seasoned and prepped and fire up the grill."

* * *

Arnold and Wesley arrived at the triangular monstrosity several miles away as the curled slice of moon rose overhead like a sickle. The intoxicating aroma of grilled meat filled the area like a wafting cloud, making Arnold want to chomp at the air.

Wesley crept to the back window and cupped his large paws against the glass to peer inside. He saw the six men drinking and laughing at the table, each with a plate containing remnants of bone and meat. Drool dribbled from his lips down the polished glass.

It had been years since he'd tasted red meat.

Not since his mother was alive.

She was a fierce predator that brought the boys *lots* to try *before she*...

"What's the plan," Arnold asked, breaking Wesley from his dreamy state. "How are we going to get them outta there?"

"There's gotta be a way to *distract* them."

They listened to the generator crank away nearby.

"What is *that*?" Arnold pointed to the generator.

"No clue. Why?"

"Because it's annoying me," Arnold snarled. "How am I supposed to *think* with that racket?"

"It isn't bothering *me*."

"Well, it's driving *me* crazy." Arnold walked over to the shed that housed the generator.

The noise was louder there.

Wesley whispered. "Wonder what it does?"

"Wanna find out?"

Wesley nodded and smiled. Arnold tore the door to the shed open.

***

Jimmy heard the shed door swing wide with a groan while the others continued to chat. Furrowing his brow, he walked over to the large windows lining the back of the lodge. He peered out into the darkness and gasped.

The bear had returned.

No, wait.

It was *two* bears. Two *big* bears.

Rummaging through the shed near the generator and breakers.

"Guys!" Jimmy turned, astounded, unsure if he was terrified, excited, or a potent mixture of both. "*Look!*"

Notches jumped up so wildly from his seat that his shot glass tipped over, spilling booze on the smoky glass tabletop. His chair toppled over, and his shamrock-green eyes lit up.

"Dibs," Notches shouted gleefully. "I got a bear tag this year!"

Jimmy joked under his breath, "Like *not having one* has ever stopped you *before*." He motioned to the taxidermied grizzly ten feet away.

Notches rolled his eyes. "You're never gonna let me live that one down, are ya?"

Jimmy opened his mouth to speak but was stopped short.

The chandelier and lamps in the lodge blinked off, then on, then off again, bathing the pyramid in the sickly off-tangerine sheen of the dwindling fire.

Zzzzzzzziiiiiinggggg.

The lights powered on again, and Jimmy watched as the grizzlies tore at the walls of the shed outside, entranced by the large steamy wafts of breath snorted from their crinkled noses.

The clients scrambled, putting on their boots. Grabbing their rifles from the upright rack by the front door.

Suddenly…

Zzzzzzzziiiiiinggggg.

Silence from the generator. The lodge went dark once again. A hush fell upon them all as the white noise dissipated and the device ceased to function.

The men headed out the side door and trampled across the wraparound porch, excitedly climbing over the handrails and dropping onto the grass one by one. They stomped into the frigid night air in a chaotic single-file line, like soldiers rushing off the ramp of a plane into battle.

They made their way around back, rifles drawn like an uncoordinated SWAT team, leaving the door wide open, heat seeping out into the chilled air.

Tom and Charles stood together in silence, secretly wishing the crescent of light above would offer more to illuminate their path.

Tom swallowed hard, worried that things could quickly go south. He didn't want to end up in the belly of a bear tonight.

The shed doors were destroyed. One hung limply from its torn upper hinges; the other was no more than shredded planks of treated pine scattered on the ground.

The commercial-grade generator was toppled over, smashed in on one side, leaking fluids onto the leaves below.

Notches had his head on a swivel, eagerly searching for the apex predators' presence, seemingly nowhere to be found.

Jimmy shivered, eyeing the massive damage the bears had done in a short time. He knew that without the generator, the temperature in the lodge would drop significantly, as would the morale of the rich clowns in his care who expected luxury for the hefty price tag he charged.

He didn't want the Yale boys to see him lose his cool, though. He still hoped that, with some extra effort and a blazing fire in the hearth, he could salvage their experience and send them away at the end of it with some wild stories and noteworthy kills so that they would send their wealthy friends his way.

The whole thing secretly rattled Jimmy to his core, though. Animals strong enough to upend a huge generator shouldn't be messed with.

SMASH!

The sound came from the front of the lodge. The shatter of glass rang out, scattering the murder of crows in a tree near the lake. They took off, cawing like giant bats against tumultuous lake waves.

"What was that?!" Jimmy suddenly wished he was armed with a weapon, too.

They all raced to the front of the peaked building just in time to see one of the grizzlies gallop down a trail that winded down the cliff-side, bounding like a beefy jackrabbit.

Notches aimed his .300 Win Mag and fired.

BOOM!

Missed.

The bear continued its trajectory, picking up the pace.

Notches looked at the clients. "What're y'all waitin' for? An invitation?"

BOOM!

BOOM!

Stan fired next, and then Chuck right after.

Mike and Tom held their fire. Tom pressed a finger to the bridge of his glasses. They fogged slightly in the cold with each panting breath.

"He's gone," Notches said, hocking a wad of phlegm into a nearby juniper.

"I've never seen a bear that *close* before." Chuck laughed nervously, gulping hard, clutching his thudding chest with his free hand. "That was *wild*."

"Yeah, well, keep your eyes peeled. There were *two*. I only saw one run into the woods. The other'n could be 'round here still."

The men turned around to see Jimmy facing the lodge, jaw wide open in shock at the damage in front of him. One of the massive windows was smashed in.

An Adirondack chair was missing from the set on the porch and now laid in the foyer on its side. There was a gaping hole in the side of the building, which now had no means of heat beyond a fireplace.

While the destruction done to the *Elk Mountain Lodge* would be costly to repair, Jimmy was equally worried about how awful the accommodations would be for the boys through the cold night.

The kitschy, jumping fish thermometer by the front door read forty degrees Fahrenheit, and it still had a long way to drop.

The men would be uncomfortable, to say the least.

Even *with* a fire.

Click.

Click.

Clickety-click-clack-click.

What is that sound, Jimmy wondered, trying to imagine what the source of the sharp noises could possibly be.

They were coming from inside the darkened building.

Jimmy ascended the steps and peered in through the shattered glass opening. Fragments of it glittered in the waning firelight, in a spray across the floor.

Jimmy's eyes caught a glimpse of something stirring inside. He reached for the pistol he usually kept by his waist out of pure muscle memory and cursed himself for not carrying it.

As he squinted, he saw what looked like a full-grown elk stuck with its head in the house's side door, unable to get his colossal rack of antlers out of the opening.

"What the…" Jimmy's eyes widened as the animal bucked and thrashed. He watched the animal whip hard and saw a piece of the antlers break off and clatter to the floor, tumbling through the kitchen.

Roooooooooaaaaaaaaaahhhhhhhhhhhhhhh!

A bear roared.

The suddenness of the powerful sound sent Jimmy running backward, crashing into the railing, nearly upending himself over it like a gymnast.

"Oh my God!" Stan clutched his chest and laughed, turning around to face the direction of the noise. He raised his 7mm Remington Magnum and stared through the scope, finger nowhere near the trigger until he located the source of the roar.

The elk disappeared into the darkness beyond the door frame, leaving nothing but a ravaged chunk of antler behind as proof that it had even happened.

Stan stealthily made his way to the corner of the patio so that he could see around the house.

The elk skittered backward into the woods.

Wait....

Backwards?

Could elk even run backward?

Stan raised his .7 Mag and aimed, firing one shot off.

BOOM!

Crack!

An explosion of bark erupted right beside the animal as it pummeled the trunk of a tree.

"We gotta work on your aim, bud," Jimmy whispered, peering around the corner with his fingers in his ears.

Stan fumed at the comment and reloaded.

Click, click...

Pause.

BOOM!

Crack! The next shot pierced a different tree just as the elk scrambled out of sight.

"I think the sight's off on this thing," Stan growled.

The other men chuckled in their huddle on the lawn, breath visibly settling like gray fog. Mike couldn't seem to stop giggling like a hyena.

"You know what?" Stan threw his hands up in the air. "I didn't see any of *you* takin' any shots."

"Well, we thought we'd let the *Master* handle it," Chuck said, cackling louder.

"Shhhhhh!" Notches had a finger to his mouth and a scowl on his face. "Shut up and listen, idiots!"

Jimmy frowned at Notches.

They'd have to have a talk about *that* later.

Among *other* things.

There was a soft rustle through the trees, and Notches raised the rifle, squinting through the scope, aiming at seemingly nothing.

"What are you--"

"*Shhhh!* What did I just *say*?" Notches whipped his head back and glared at the offender. After a moment, he went back to peering through the magnified lens. He focused his eye on a clearing up the path a ways. It was a long shot, but if the elk or the bear came through that way, he'd be ready.

Something galloped through the narrow window he'd been focused on as if on cue.

Something dark, with horns.

Racing *backward.*

He fired. *BOOM!*

His bullet hit the target, but instead of a wounded elk bugling, a bear erupted in pain instead.

Rooooooooooooooooohhhhhhhhhhhh!

The sound was chilling.

The shot had landed.

The bear collapsed, and down came the antlers, slamming hard into a nearby tree with an audible *crack.*

Notches lowered the gun slowly, eyes wide with confusion.

"Oh my God, you hit it! What a *shot*!" Mike howled in celebration, slamming his palm on the shooter's back in congratulations. "I didn't even see the *bear* from back here. I wasn't sure *what* you were doin'."

Notches looked dazed, his eyes flitting up to Jimmy. "I think I hit a bear, but… I was aiming at an elk. I don't understand. It looked like it was runnin' in reverse."

Notches raised his gun again, and Jimmy dodged the trajectory, steering well clear of the man's aim.

"Yeah, I coulda' sworn I saw that too. I've never seen one run backward before."

"I don't think they *do*." Notches whispered, staring through the sight. He watched the black blob shifting in the moonlight and saw the antlers raise again, as if…

As if the bear was *carrying* them.

* * *

Arnold felt a searing pain in his shoulder. His arm ached and felt like it was becoming numb. Something was lodged inside of him, something radiating pain with every lift of his arm.

There was a noise in the trees ahead, and Arnold stopped in his tracks, standing in silence, hoping the humans hadn't followed him.

The steady, heavy crunch of dead branches grew louder as Arnold held his breath.

Out of the trees came a figure at least six feet tall. Arnold prepared to run, worried that this had all been for naught. Worried that he'd made a *fatal* mistake.

As a tiny sliver of moonlight lit the figure, he felt the overwhelming urge to collapse with relief.

He smiled, tears in his eyes. "Oh, am I glad to see *you*, or *what*?"

"I thought they got you, brother." Wesley was choked up. "I heard the *boom-sticks*. I thought you--" His breath hitched as he fought the urge to sob.

"I'm wounded." Arnold winced through the intense pain. "I can't believe you went through the *window* like that."

"I can't believe you used the *door*," Wesley snickered and sniffled.

Arnold stepped forward into the light. "I didn't get mom, but--"

He held up the mount of the mighty elk, glass eyes shimmering beneath the aligned stars. He offered the taxidermied head to his older brother like a macabre gift. A forked prong of antlers was missing from the left side.

"He's a little worse for wear, but... I got Big Bob."

39

The hunters inspected the damage done to the lodge. Notches was still stunned by the events that had taken place. Jimmy walked around with a flashlight, picking up overturned furniture and sweeping shattered glass.

As he returned the dustpan to the kitchen, he saw the pronged piece of broken antler lying on the floor. He picked it up and tapped it in his palm, thinking about how bizarre the sighting had been.

How did that thing even get in here? Through the busted window?

And why was it running backward?

He exhaled deeply and walked back, still gripping the antler in his fist when, finally, it occurred to him where the prong came from.

And why the animal ran in the wrong direction.

He turned, and his eyes settled on the bare spot above the fireplace where the mounted elk's head once sat.

Bare wall.

He didn't blink.

He just stared at the space where the illegally acquired trophy had been.

"Well, this sucks. Power's out. Window's *permanently* open. Gonna be a cold night," Tom exclaimed with his arms crossed as he surveyed the area.

"Thank you, *Captain Obvious*." Notches was in a snarky mood again and downed two more shots of bourbon in quick succession.

"*Nick*," Jimmy said sternly. He didn't follow up with anything, but the look in his eyes and the usage of Notches's real name made the man clam up.

"Glad I brought my long *underwear*," Chuck sniggered.

"I can't believe the size of those bears. They were huge," Tom absentmindedly pressed the bridge of his glasses, shoving them against his round face.

"You sure you didn't kill that one in the woods, man?" Stan asked Notches, pointing outside. "I can go track it down if you want."

"Nah." Notches shook his head, staring at the last remnants of booze swishing around the crystal bottle, still in disbelief. "Wasn't a kill shot. Think I just winged it."

Ryan lay alone and awake in a soft bed of leaves, too anxious to even dream of sleeping. He was wracked with guilt over the tragic loss of Kenna. She was one of their own. He felt helpless like he had somehow failed her.

His best friend was in mourning. What could he *possibly* say to make Edward feel any better.

And what of the rest of them? What about Star? What about the animals he'd grown up with, ones who still sang his father's praises?

If they perished, too…

Then what?

Soon, a battle would ensue, and its outcome would mean life or death.

He didn't have much in the way of a formalized plan to save their land and their *loved ones.*

Ryan knew that, with the presence of the humans, there would surely be more death, just as there had been today.

And what about Star? *What would he do if he lost her?* He couldn't bear the thought.

***

Ross came to Heather's treetop home after his soldiers, save for the squirrels on *Watchman's Line*, had gone to bed for the night.

He hoped to convince her to leave for a while. He wanted her kept safe during all this madness. He'd developed feelings for her, though he didn't dare tell her that.

After all, it was foolish to think that they could be together. *She should be with someone her own kind.* That's the thought he always chanted to himself as if that made his feelings for her diluted.

It didn't.

As time grew, he found he only wanted to be around her more. He delighted in her comforting nature and effortless beauty.

And her sense of humor…

Well, it was becoming harder to control his laughter around her as the days passed.

He was fairly certain she had no romantic interest in him. After all, such a union would be preposterous. But it didn't stop him from dreaming about her every night from the cubby in his rotten pine. Nor did it stop him from thinking about her in the day, as he often glimpsed her on the sidelines of his training grounds, bringing fruit to his hard-working soldiers.

"I think you should leave with the other women and young tomorrow. Just for a little while until the timbers are safe again."

She looked around for a moment, a little stunned by the caring tone of his voice. "Will you be alright?"

"Of course," he lied with confidence, having no idea if he would live or die. "I've grown up with all of these animals. I have to do something. I have to act. I must make the Great Timbers a safe place for our children."

He thought about his wording and stammered to backtrack.

"I-I-I don't necessarily mean *our* children. I mean, we don't--"

"I don't want anything to happen to you, Ross." Melancholy filled the red squirrel's giant eyes. "Please, Ross, be careful."

There was so much feeling in her words.

Like she wanted to say more.

Like she *had* to say more.

Like it was eating her up to *not* say it.

Ross grabbed Heather's chin and tilted it up towards him.

Touching her felt electric, like the pulse of something meaningful in his fingertips. He brushed a tear from her fur with his soft, black hand, then kissed her.

"I will." He could only manage a whisper.

Ross pulled away and collected himself, wanting to apologize for the forwardness of the act. But as he opened his mouth to speak…

He saw she was smiling.

Without so much as another chitter, he left the treetop home and scuttled into the cold, dark night with his heart warmed.

***

Wesley paced beside the treeline, his heart pounding, claws fidgeting nervously. "I'm fine, Ryan."

Ryan danced around in place, burning off nervous energy, "You're *not* fine. They *shot* you!"

"It's fine. It doesn't hurt that bad anymore," the grizzly said reassuringly, trying to sound tough.

"Just a little further down the path," Arnold said, motioning with his head for Ryan to follow again.

Ryan followed. Wesley followed in the rear, clutching his wound.

At the bottom of the path, Ryan froze, stone still, the moment he saw a massive rack of antlers peeking around the sides of a tree.

"What's with the antlers on the ground? Are those sheds?" He finally took a timid step toward them.

"No." Arnold rubbed the back of his neck with his black palm. There was a melancholic look about him, one that made the elk uneasy.

"Did… you kill one of our kind?" Ryan's eyes were large, begging it to not be true.

"What? No!" Wesley interjected.

"No…" Arnold muttered. "It's your father, Ryan."

Wesley picked up the mount of Big Bob carefully. Ryan stared at it and swallowed down the hard lump in his throat.

"You… risked your lives to steal back my father?" Ryan asked, his voice sounded distant, smaller.

"We tried to rescue our mother, too, but…" His voice drifted off as if in a bizarre dream he couldn't seem to wake from.

"How did you get this?" Ryan was horrified.

"From the triangle," Wesley said.

Silence.

Not a sound was made beyond the far-away hoot of the old owl.

"We didn't think it was right, Ryan." Arnold looked at the elk with glassy eyes.

Ryan swallowed hard again, trying to find his voice in the pain. "Thank you." His gaze fell to the forest floor, then to his father's face, eyes wide with a far-away look. "I will never forget this."

***

Hours later, on what would surely be a sleepless night, Ryan, Ross, Arnold, and Wesley gathered in the meadow with the moles and ever-growing family of groundhogs around the freshly dug pit that now held Big Bob's mount.

"May you finally rest in peace, Father," Ryan said, fighting to stay strong through the rushing waves of emotion. "We shall look up to you, just as we *always* did, and know that you are there, watching over us, as the brightest star in the *Alignment*."

With that, Ryan nodded to Wesley and Arnold as they scooped mounds of loose dirt into the hole, finally giving the mighty leader the sendoff he so rightly deserved.

41

Chuck's phone alarm chimed at four a.m., just a few short, freezing hours after the men had gone to bed. He sat up and looked around at the others, who were also groggily shifting, hesitant to rise.

"Ahh, you're up. Finally, I can do this," Jimmy said from atop a ladder in the main room, salesman grin plastered on his face. He tore off a piece of duct tape with a loud *shiiiiiiink!*

He pressed a sheet of painter's plastic against the windows and taped one corner up. He pulled it taut across the gaping hole and stuck a tacky piece to the other corner.

"Thank God the crew that did the floors left these. This outta help a little." He hopped off the ladder and tended to the lower corners as the men shook the sleep from their eyes.

Chuck shivered. The frosty air had penetrated the lodge in an undeniable way, making it tougher to get ready for the day's excursion. He rubbed his arms to warm himself despite the presence of the blazing fire roaring away in the red stone fireplace below.

The men donned their long underwear and woodland camouflage, putting their hunter-orange accessories on last. They gathered their boots, rifles, and ammunition and filled their thermoses with piping-hot coffee.

Notches stared back at Mike and Chuck as he swallowed a mouthful of banana bread. "I'm taking y'all to a *really* special spot today, boys. It's where I took down 'at beast." He pointed to the mounted bear by the fireplace. "Hope you're ready for the hunt of your *life*."

42

Ryan and Ross surveyed the area when the first sign of daylight filtered through the trees, the raccoon on his antlers for an optimal view.

"Are you ready for this?" Ryan asked.

"Ready as I ever *could* be," Ross replied. "Do you think the humans will come?"

"Bet on it," Ryan firmly said, then ground his molars. "If I should die, Ross… I'd like to be buried next to my father."

"Don't talk like that." Ross crossed his arms in front of his dark gray chest. Ross shuddered to think about it. Years ago, they were strangers. Now, they were *family*.

Ryan had his doubts about their survival. If the humans could take down his father and Kilgore without so much as breaking a *sweat*…

What *else* were they capable of?

Rumors of Kilgore's body, frozen like his father's head, chilled him more than any Wyoming wind ever could.

What if they were *next*…

Next to be frozen in place, posing eternally for the entertainment of humans.

43

Notches and the clients were glassing from the ridge, searching for signs of life. Bright sparkles of dawn's light danced off the dew and frost-covered meadow below.

"I'm tellin' ya, this place is crawlin' with wildlife. You'll see," Notches whispered to Mike, adjusting his neon-orange beanie.

"We're gonna do a little pushin', boys. When we get to the bottom of the ridge, we're gonna split up. Mike, you take Chuck and Stan and walk along the east side of the meadow into those pines. Nerd-boy and I'll walk along the west bank over 'ere by the stream. We're gonna go in first. You boys stay on the outskirts at the ready if we miss or spook somethin' out your way. After a bit, we'll switch."

Notches set his backpack in the dirt, in the spot where he'd knocked Mickey out cold long ago. He suppressed a smile at the thought and handed each man a walkie-talkie. "We're on channel three. Don't radio 'less you need serious help, or you bagged somethin' big, *got it?* Keep the channel open and the volume as low as possible."

The men nodded in understanding of the rules and carefully started down the side of the treacherous ridge.

***

Edgar fluttered down, perching on a branch between Ross and Ryan, pointed backward at the edge of the timbers.

"Ross, there's something you should know," he squawked, facing the pine tree.

"I'm over here, you *do-do* bird. Turn around," Ross snapped and then looked at Ryan. "I can't believe we trust intel from this guy."

"Yes, of course," Edgar ignored the comment. Then, his eyes bulged in a sudden look of panic. "Humans are near! I saw them near the ridge."

Ryan's eyes widened, too. "How many?"

"Five."

"Wait, weren't there *six* before?" Ross scrunched his black eyebrows.

"Yes, one might be back inside the human's triangle. But on the ridge, there were only five. I counted twice."

Ross flashed Ryan a look as if to say, *I don't know how much we should trust this moron.*

But Ryan's eyes were fixed on something past him, deep in thought, imagining his next move.

"Alright, it's time."

"Aye, aye!" Ross stood at attention.

44

Mike walked ahead of Chuck and Stan as the three men made their way along the edge of the meadow, cautiously watching for signs of wild game. There were tracks in the soft dirt. Mike stopped to look at them.

As he knelt next to the prints, he heard a noise in the trees. He eyed Chuck and Stan, wondering if they'd heard it too.

They *had*.

The men listened for the sound to repeat.

The branches of the pines in the treeline moved as if the row of trees were waving at them. But that was impossible.

Wasn't it?

Mike pointed his rifle toward the rustling pines and moved closer.

Suddenly, a young fawn came trotting out from behind some trees.

"Aww," Mike whispered, "look at him." He looked back to the others.

They seemed unimpressed.

The fawn was much too young to hunt. They were saving their tags for something mature.

"Hello, little guy," Chuck said quietly as the deer walked right up to them. "Is your *papa* around here?"

"Or your *mama*," Stan added.

"Well, wherever there's a lil' one, an adult won't be too far away," whispered Chuck as he looked around the trees.

"Hey, look at this!" Mike grinned from ear to ear. "This little guy likes me. Look, he's waggin' his tail."

"He's not a *dog*, you idiot."

"I wonder why he's coming up to us. Aren't they supposed to be, you know, skittish around humans," Chuck asked, brow furrowed.

Mike dropped to his knees and spoke sweetly. "Hi."

The fawn walked right up to him, investigated him with his nose, and then turned around.

Mike made a face, one to show how excited he was at the close interaction.

Without warning, the fawn reared his leg forward and kicked Mike hard in the face with all its might.

Mike groaned loudly and fell to the ground, clutching his jaw. "He *kicked* me! *Hard*! You little…"

Mike lunged at the deer.

He didn't have a plan of what he'd do if he *caught* it. But he didn't catch the whitetail. The fawn was too fast and jetted out from his grasp, escaping narrowly, then slowing down as if to taunt the man.

A moment later, the deer took off, running into the woods.

Mike raised his rifle.

Chuck shoved the barrel of it to the ground. "What are you *doing*, Mike? That thing's a *baby*! Don't be an idiot."

"Maybe he'll lead us to a bigger one, though. Where there's a baby, there's usually a parent nearby, right?" Chuck laughed nervously, unsure if that was actually correct.

Mike nodded to him, rubbing the tender spot on his mandible where the fawn kicked him. He could already feel a bruise forming.

Stan looked up into the trees and saw a swarm of rodents watching them from the trees.

"Wow, Notches wann't kiddin' about this place being loaded with animals."

He looked up at them again, swarming on boughs in organized lines.

And did one of them have a rock in its hand?

***

"Right flank, attack!" Ross gave the signal from a bough near the center to the other tree creatures.

Nuts and rocks showered down out of the trees from their right, smacking them in the skulls, thwacking them in the eyes and chests like hail.

"Left flank, attack!"

A barrage of painful granite and quartz fired off from the left, hitting the men with accuracy and precision.

Ross grabbed a stone and hurled it at Mike, striking him right in the temple with a resounding *whack*!

The man saw a flash of white and felt blood trickle down the side of his face. He looked back up at the raccoon, tender jaw taut with anger.

"*What's going on?!*" One of the men whipped his head around, astounded by the shower of fist and marble-sized projectiles.

Two of the more cowardly men rushed deeper into the woods when they saw the creatures gearing up to launch more rocks and nuts. They were vastly outnumbered by the animals. Heading into the woods seemed to be the quickest way out of the path of their rocky rain.

"Right flank, attack!"

More animals further down to the right of the worn path fired, hurling stones, walnuts, and hazelnuts as far as their arms would allow.

Ross picked up a stone the size of a golf ball and hurled it at the human again, smacking him square in the back of the skull.

The man jolted forward and fell to his knees.

"Left flank, attack!"

The left fired again, letting loose another barrage of excruciatingly painful gravel.

The lone man covered his face as the storm of rocks and nuts pounded him mercilessly.

Once they had fallen, he growled loudly, no longer afraid of scaring away any nearby game.

Furious, the man raised his rifle and aimed at Ross, squinting through the scope.

"Look out, Ross," an opossum screamed, drooling out the sides of his wide lips from the anxiety of the situation.

Ross hurled himself from his spot on the branch a mere moment before the bullet ripped through the tree bark where he'd once stood.

Ross tumbled from the bough, smashing down on the one below, losing his balance, and smashing into another.

"No," a young squirrel kit screamed from a few trees over, watching the scene.

From where he stood, it looked like Ross was hit.

Ross looked up from the bough that caught his fall and shook his head. His small body had been battered by the fall.

The hunter took aim at the masked critter…

"Look out," another squirrel shouted at the top of his lungs.

The hunter was so focused on shooting the varmint that he didn't see Herbie approach again. With his eyes squinted to protect from the rock rain, he hadn't seen the fawn spin and rear his leg, smashing it into the tender crook of the man's thigh, near his groin.

The gun went off again, this time into the sky, and the man dropped to his knees.

Wasting no time at all, Herbie kicked him again, *hard*, in the chest.

***

Chuck and Stan trampled on each other, trying to scramble back the way they came.

The hiss of the walkie sounded.

"What in God's name is going *on* over there!"

It was Notches.

"You'd *better* have shot something because you just scared off the elk Tom and I just found!"

The static dissipated.

Then the voice came back over the airwaves. "It was a big one, too!"

Mike, bruised and bleeding, stuffed his hand in his pocket and fished out his walkie, still flinching as if he'd be pummeled by more pebbles and rocks. "Notches, something *weird* is going on over here--"

Mike sounded like he was fighting the urge to bawl. Injured and confused, he pressed himself against the trunk of a jack pine and struggled to find the right words to describe his situation to the guide.

Beneath his fingers, he could feel deep gouges and striations made by nightmarish bear claws.

"I--" Just as Mike started to speak again, he looked straight up and immediately wished he hadn't.

Forty feet up, in the towering tree overhead, a squirrel, a weasel, and an opossum had their tiny paws against different sides of a cinder block-sized rock, teetering on a branch barely thick enough to hold the weight. Spanning a foot and a half wide, it was a struggle to hold, even with their group effort.

Before Mike could bolt away, the raccoon chittered, and the animals released.

The large rock tumbled over the edge of the bough and careened through the air before he could register what he was seeing.

The lump of granite filling his field of vision was the last thing he ever saw.

With the force of the bludgeon, Mike died instantly. The sickening crunch rang out through the forest.

His body lay still, bloodied and unmoving, as the morning sun broke the horizon, pouring in through the trees in golden ribbons.

45

Chuck and Stan desperately tried to find their way back to the meadow. Driven by fear, the men ran past the trees, stumbling, pushing branches aside as they ran.

Suddenly, Stan heard a noise from the trees next to the trail they were following. Gawking at the forest around him for the throngs of tiny nut-chuckers, Chuck tripped and tumbled to the ground.

Stan grabbed Chuck by the bright orange vest and yanked him up. "I think we're being followed."

"It's probably Mike," Chuck grumbled as he brushed off his pants and coat.

"Did you *see* that? I've never seen animals act like that before!"

Another noise sounded from the trees.

This time, Chuck heard it too.

Both men loaded their rifles and looked around.

"Mike?"

They waited for a moment, hoping Mike would emerge from a thicket.

"Mike? That *you*?"

"Mike, this seriously is not the time for a practical joke."

There was no reply.

The bushes rustled beside them, and Chuck jumped away. He aimed his barrel at the foliage.

Something darted out with a hissing *swoosh,* and Chuck, scared by the abrupt appearance, fired immediately.

The creature dropped.

Stan laughed nervously. He wasn't sure what *at.*

Just… *everything*, he supposed. This had gone from a relaxing trip to a totally surreal experience in a matter of twenty minutes.

The bush stopped moving.

A small, hoofed leg pressed out.

Chuck cautiously pushed the branches away with the end of his rifle.

There, he saw the fawn that had kicked Mike lying on the ground.

Struck in its chest.

A vital shot.

The men stood silent, watching it perish.

The fawn looked up at the men with bulbous, sad eyes, twitched in pain, and stopped breathing.

46

"Aww, man, what a waste of a tag. That thing's tiny."

"Mike'll be excited, though," Chuck mumbled with disappointment, pulling out his walkie. He held it to his face and hesitated to push the button. His mouth hung open, and he thought for a moment. "*Heyyyyy...*"

Stan raised his eyebrows, still staring at the fawn. "Yeah?"

"What *if...*" Chuck hesitated, "And I'm only *spitballin'* here. What if... we just like, you know, pushed it under the bush? Leave it for the coyotes."

"That's risky, Chucky. You get caught abandoning it--"

"Yeah, but like..." Chuck trailed off and grunted petulantly.

"Where's Mike?" Stan whispered, staring off in the direction they came, the area of rock rain. "I'm startin' to get worried about him."

"Should we radio him?"

Stan shrugged. "Wouldn't hurt."

Chuck leaned his back against a tree, depressed the button, and held the plastic walkie to his lips, closer than he needed to. "Mike, you okay?"

Silence.

Then… Notches.

"What did I *say* about stayin' off the airwaves 'less it's an emergency?"

"I think it might be." Chuck swallowed hard and looked at Stan, both enveloped by the eerie silence of the woods.

From the other end, Notches let out a staticky sigh and then said, "Michael? You good, bud?"

Nothing.

Silence, again.

"Mike, do you hear us? Answer, man."

Nothing still.

Then, around the men, came another noise:

The windy rustle of leaves…

Without the presence of wind itself.

Chuck looked around, on high alert, and reloaded the chamber of his Springfield.

A smattering of bark tinkled down on his painfully orange baseball cap.

He looked up.

"What the--"

Stan craned his neck to see what Chuck was reacting to.

High up in the jack pine, above him, a full-grown grizzly clung to the trunk, staring down at him.

Before Chuck could raise his rifle, the bear released his arms from around the trunk and careened straight down, balling his body into a 600-pound fur-coated boulder.

Stan heard Chuck's neck crack on impact, crumpling the stout man's body into a rumpled mound of skin and shattered bone.

There was no way for the man to survive the crushing force as it devastated his form and the tender organs inside in an instant.

The bear stood, leaving the deceased hunter in a tangled mound of motionless limbs and bloodied camo fabric.

The walkie was shattered, a crumpled mess of circuit boards and cheap plastic parts.

ROOOUUOOOOAAHHHHHHHH!

The bear belched a fierce growl and stared at the man who shot him just hours before.

Stan openly wept, unable to bring his hands to function in the face of the beast before him.

Standing two feet away, he couldn't even raise his gun without stepping backward.

Instead, he blubbered and urinated in his pants, trembling in fear.

"P-P-Please! Plllleeeeeee-e-e-ease!"

It wasn't a full sentence, but the pathetic pleading sounds would have to suffice as his last words.

The bear whipped his uninjured arm and thrashed the shuddering man, clawing the flesh of his throat and face in one swipe. Stan flew into the jack pine with the devastating force of the swing. The grizzly pounced, shredding the man with powerful jaws until he was nothing but a writhing mess on the mulched forest floor.

He reached for his walkie and held it to his mouth. But as he pressed the button, the only sound he could make was a wet gurgle before one final dying gasp.

47

Wesley caught his breath and licked the warm, crimson liquid off his gargantuan paws. It had been years since he had eaten red meat. It tasted foreign to him now. He'd grown accustomed to the sweet, flaky taste of rainbow trout and crawfish, unable to remember the last time Kilgore had brought him and Arnold a bloody kill to feast on.

Despite looking like mashed raspberries, the fluid on him tasted even sweeter…

It tasted like *revenge*.

Once he'd had his fill of the feast before him, Wesley licked his wet, red snout and walked over to the spot where poor Herbie had been slain. He stared down at the young deer, thinking about the sad cruelty of the situation.

He picked the small body up and carried the lolling fawn deep into the Great Timbers to a serene spot, far from the corpses of the humans.

Unlike them, he figured the little chap deserved a proper burial if they survived this.

48

Notches happened upon a large fallen timber and knelt beside it, gasping almost imperceptibly at the sight before him. Tom squatted next to him, and both men watched a moving object in the woods through their scopes.

"Oh, my, would you lookie *here*." Notches had a broad-shouldered buck in his scope, but it was still too far away to squeeze off a good shot.

No.

Tom, he reminded himself.

For *Tom* to squeeze off a good shot.

Notches was constantly forgetting that he was in the woods to guide the Yale boys to a kill…

Not to get one for himself.

But a man could *dream,* couldn't he?

"Look at the *size* of this guy," Notches whispered. "He's *huge*."

Tom eyed the animal through his scope. "He's an eight-point buck, massive rack, huge tines."

Notches nodded, green eyes affixed with an obsessive gaze. He whispered, "Eight-point buck. Must be a *New England* thing. 'Round here, we call 'at a *four-by-four*."

An eagle circling the air above them screeched.

SCREEEEEEEEEE!

The buck turned his head in their direction, almost as if he could see Notches and Tom from a great distance.

Both men sat perfectly still for a moment.

Notches whispered, "You're probably only gonna get one shot. Breathe deep. Make it count."

"I've hunted *before*," Tom whispered back snidely, glaring at his guide through the corners of his eyes.

"Sorry, city boy. My bad." But Notches wasn't sorry. "It's just… if it weren't for seein' you kill that doe yesterday with my own two eyes, the way y'all were shootin' at that bear last night, I wasn't sure any of you'd ever gotten a kill before."

His tone made Tom's skin crawl.

"Now," the man took a breath, "*go on*. Git yourself a mantle mount."

Tom stared at the whitetail deer through the crosshairs of his scope.

Notches plugged his ears, narrowed his wrinkled eyes, and waited eagerly for the young man to pull the trigger.

49

Jimmy took a sip of his coffee, so full of cream and sugar that it no longer resembled anything of the sort. He stared up at the painter's plastic taped to the hole in the front of his brand-new lodge.

In retrospect, maybe the more expensive tempered glass would've been the way to go, he thought, *at least for the first row of windows. But then again, hindsight always was 20/20.*

Keeka padded over, brushed affectionately against his side, and panted.

"Ugh." He shoved her away with his knee. "Get offa me. You're shedding like *crazy*."

Keeka walked into the living room, dejected, and lay at the foot of the standing grizzly. She stared up with her sad, blue eyes and softly patted her fluffy tail on the rug.

Just beyond the plastic, some moving forms caught Jimmy's eye, bokeh blobs of darkness set against a dusky, dandelion-yellow backdrop as the sun crept over the lake.

Jimmy cocked his head to the side with curiosity and walked around the plastic toward the front door, tugging it open carefully, unsure if the frame's structure was compromised by the shattered window.

He gasped.

Outside, a hoard of animals had swarmed the arctic-white side-by-side, each taking its devastating toll on the vehicle. Squirrels and marmots chewed the seats. A pair of raccoons scuttled out from underneath, covered in fluids, splashing their black paws in a puddle of what looked like oil.

A family of groundhogs had gnawed through the back tire, a feat Jimmy imagined must've taken hours.

"Get outta here!" Jimmy screamed out the open doorway in a booming voice.

But the animals didn't scatter. They barely budged, stopping in their tracks to look at him, dropping whatever they had in their mouths or tiny hands.

"Go on! Git!" Jimmy rushed down the stairs and kicked a hunk of dry dirt at them. It dissipated in the air a few feet away like an orange-tinged firework.

An owl hooted, loud and clear.

The creatures scurried in different directions, scattering into the brush near the shore of the lake.

Craaaaaaaaaaack-SNAP!

The sound of wood breaking came a split second before Jimmy saw it.

A massive pine tree toppling over like a backward pendulum.

He darted to the house just in time for--

WHAMMMMMM!

SMASSSSSSSSSH!

Shattered glass exploded everywhere. Wood planks flew and smashed. Foliage shot up in a chaotic spray. Keeka shot toward the back of the house, trembling.

A fallen tree took out the entire front of the house, crushing everything in its path from the windows to the porch. Jimmy looked up from the floor, which glistened like fractals of scattered ice all around him.

He could have been killed!

The downed tree sat in front of him as if it had always been there as if the lodge had been built *around* it somehow.

The *Elk Mountain Lodge* was in shambles, and he suddenly wondered about his insurance policy's strength and his trusting investors' disapproval.

The beaver took a few steps toward him, snapping him out of his pragmatic thoughts and worries. He rapidly whacked his flattened tail on the ground.

Thump-thump-thump thump-thump!

As if this were a cue, the other woodland creatures raced toward him.

He let out a scream inadvertently, one that arose over Keeka's warning barks. He scrambled back, feeling the tiny shards of glass as they dug into his palms.

The army of fur-coated animals piled into the house…

And ran amok.

***

"Destroy everything!" Richard raised his oily hand up into the air as he screamed.

And the creatures all went to work, gnawing furniture, shredding bedding, scrambling through kitchen cabinets, upending foodstuffs, and ruthlessly scattering the hunter's personal effects across the floor.

Gophers burrowed deep holes in the brand-new L-shaped couch, shooting cotton from the craters until the floor looked like it was covered in clouds.

"What can I do?" Keeka barked, drawing the human's eyes to her. "I want to help you stop them, once and for all!"

Richard saw the wild look in her eyes and grinned. "*Well, well.* Looks like you can take the wolf outta the *wild,* but you can't take the *wild* outta the *wolf.*" He winked.

Keeka took a few steps toward him and barked again, bouncing as she did. "Put me to work!"

"Well, find yourself a spot, little lady, and get to devastatin'!"

Keeka walked over to the glass table, stood beneath it, and rose to her hind legs, using the flat spot on the top of her head to launch the table on its side.

CRASH!

It cracked into jagged, smoky shards, splaying across the floor.

"Atta girl!" Richard giggled and then pointed a black finger at the human. "*Langston*! It's time!"

Langston, a gray squirrel, popped his head out of a cereal box, spit out his sugar-coated bran, and galloped over to the human, scaling his clothes quickly as if he were a tree.

The human screamed, which brought joy to the squirrel's heart. He perched on the man's shoulder, dodging his wild, flailing hands, and sunk his unforgiving teeth down through the human's ear.

The human roared and swung again.

The next thing Langston knew, he was in the air, careening toward a marble countertop. He landed but couldn't get traction, and despite his scramble to stay on, he slid off onto the floor.

Richard doubled over with laughter. "Good work!" He looked around. "Now, the other squirrels!"

The human clutched his bleeding ear and saw a sea of black, beady eyes, all twisting toward him at once.

As the creatures raced toward him in unison, the human bolted for the bathroom and shut the door just as he heard the thud-thud-thud of their bodies against the wood.

Langston flattened to the floor, mushing his face against the crack beneath.

"What's he doing?" A red squirrel whispered.

The human ran his hands through his sparse hair and laughed incredulously. He looked in the mirror and examined the streak of blood he'd accidentally smeared from his ear into his blond locks.

"Everyone..." Langston narrowed his eyes, "*chew!*"

As the others continued to devastate the *Elk Mountain Lodge*, the battalion of squirrels all formed a row at the bottom of the bathroom door and began to gnaw at the wood.

The horrendous sound echoed through the open space, rising over the beaver's non-stop laughter.

50

Tom focused through the scope, taking a deep breath. His index finger touched the cold steel of the trigger.

That buck was going *down*.

He was about to be two-for-two on this excursion, a point of great pride for the oft-bullied man.

He locked the buck's chest cavity between the cross.

SCREEEEEE!

Tom didn't know what hit him. Something hard clubbed him in the side of the head, and all he saw was brown feathers flapping in his face.

BOOM!

He fired, much by accident, missing the buck by several feet. The whitetail jetted off, and Notches fumbled with the creature as it pecked at them with its powerful beak.

SCREE! SCREEEEEEEE!

The sound the thing made was at a pitch that felt deafening to the men. Notches leaned back, hands in the dirt, and used his hiking boot to shove the bird off.

The massive wingspan caught both men repeatedly as it flapped.

Tom screamed.

Notches saw, amid the flurry of chocolate-brown wings, that Tom was bleeding from several holes pecked into his face.

"Get it off me!" His shrieks of terror continued for a moment, and the bird took off with a tremendous bolt of power, soaring straight into the sky.

Tom scrambled for his rifle and aimed at the avian. Notches tackled him.

"Are you crazy? Those are an endangered species. I am not going down for your stupidity, you hear me?" As he heard the words replay in his head, the irony of the situation was not lost on him.

"That thing destroyed my face!" Tom screeched, nearly as loud as the bird had.

"Quit your whinin'. You'll be fine. Those are flesh wounds. Plus," Notches hit him in the arm, attempting to be friendly, "chicks dig scars. And now you can tell people you wrestled with a bald eagle. Not every'un can say that! I'll back you up."

Up ahead, the buck kicked up a pile of leaves, strutting in a way that almost looked like he was taunting the armed men.

"Hey!" Notches whispered, pointing, "Guess who you didn't scare off?"

The buck stared them down momentarily and then took off straight down the path. Still infuriated by the eagle attack, Tom stood up, pointed his gun, and tromped through the woods after it.

Notches followed behind, gun and pack slung over his back, rolling his eyes at Tom.

Chasing an animal through the woods? Clearly, he hadn't hunted much.

Why not just fire off an air horn to announce yourself?

As Tom's pace quickened, the whitetail skittered another twenty-or-so feet and then paused and looked back, almost like he was beckoning. Then he galloped another twenty, craning his neck again.

Tom was ready, rifle poised, eye glancing more through the scope than at the ground.

The buck made its way to a curving path that trailed up a hill with a flattened top.

Whoosh-whoosh!

The sound came from overhead.

But Tom was more preoccupied by the sight at his feet. He had nearly walked into a deep pit, one whose bottom was filled with sharpened sticks, all buried in the ground, pointing skyward.

"Tom, look out!" Notches hollered.

The deer took off.

As Tom turned in place to find out what Notches was screaming about, it was too late. The bald eagle careened full force into his chest as if trying to fly through him.

It smashed into him and knocked him backward. Tom was airborne for only a split second before he felt the wooden spikes pierce right through his chest, pelvis, right arm, and left leg, locking him in place.

His lung deflated, and he gasped for air. Moments later, his mouth filled with blood, and what should have been shooting pain was replaced by adrenaline and shock.

He coughed, wet and quiet, unable to speak.

The eagle carried on, soaring high into the sky above.

Notches watched the whole thing in absolute horror, terrified at what he had just witnessed and what it meant for Jimmy's business. He was supposed to protect these yuppies. Now, he was about to be out of a job.

Nausea swelled in him, and he fought the urge to vomit at the sight of Tom's body as he took his final breath. The man's face and glasses were spattered in ruby fluid.

Notches looked up at the butte before him, awed by the sight of a massive elk standing at the top near the whitetail buck Tom had chased to his demise.

The elk snorted angrily and raised his head high. His bugle escalated to a long, whistling squeal punctuated by an aggressive grunt. The buck and bull started down the path, eyes locked on Notches.

He couldn't shake the feeling that they were coming to get him.

As the mammals picked up speed, their gaze never leaving his face…

He realized…

They *were*.

51

Jimmy watched the hole in the bottom of the door widen. Little arms, legs, tips of tails, and orange-tinged teeth crept out of it like some tiny mutant monstrosity that was all limbs and hungry mouths. He knew soon the gap would be wide enough for them to funnel in. He looked around. No windows. Little in the way of weapons.

He grabbed a plunger, knelt down, and shoved the handle of it through the hole, wriggling it back and forth to whack away the rodents.

Grrrrrrrrrrrrrrrnnnnnnnnnnnnnnnnn-grnnnn.

Grrrrrrrrrrrrrnnnnnnnn-grnnnn-grunnnn.

The noise sounded like metal on wood, clattering, groaning.

"Notches? Is that you?!"

He listened.

Nothing but the sound again.

Grrrrrrrrrrrrnnnnnnnn-grnnnn-grunnnn.

Whatever it was, it was *big*.

SMASH.

More glass breaking. Somewhere near the fireplace.

The clatter continued, and Jimmy kicked at the hole in the door to stop the chewing momentarily.

"Guys, I'm in the bathroom! Is that you?"

BAM!

The sound of something massive flipping. Then...

Clomp.

Clomp.

Clomp.

Clomp.

BAM!

Something big was inside, moving furniture.

Silence. The squirrels stopped chewing. He heard their little feet scuttle away in droves.

He peered through the hole they had gnawed, unnerved by the sight of a wide bear's foot coming into view.

Then *grinding*.

Wood on wood.

Followed by a horrendous thump that rattled the whole bathroom. Something slammed up against the door. He looked through the hole again, but the view was obscured. All he saw was cotton and gray fabric eclipsing the light.

Rising to his knees, he sniffed, face twisted into a contorted look of horror.

Is that… smoke?

***

Ryan and Edward raced through the forest, watching the human stumble over fallen logs and trip on uneven ground.

They maintained their pace, toying with the man.

"You go back and check on the others." Ryan motioned for Edward to make the trek to the pyramid. "This one's *mine*."

The gusts were brutal, knocking him about like an unseen giant's hand, but the gallop of the hooves behind him kept him motivated.

***

Notches burst into the clearing, looking around the meadow, feeling his pockets for his walkie-talkie. He found it, never stopping, and rushed across the meadow, legs moving like a former track star, lungs heaving like a heavy smoker.

The cold air burned with every inhale, and the southeastern wind slapped him from the side.

Still, he picked himself up, rarely looking back, focused on the worn path leading up the hill to the plateau and the route back to safety.

Notches held the walkie up to his mouth and depressed the button, barely able to form words through the wheezing.

"Jim--" He panted. "Jim, I need help."

Silence.

"Jim, for God's sake, HELP me!"

***

"Jim, for God's sake, HELP me!" The unattended walkie sounded from the broken wood and glass spray on the foyer floor.

Nearby, Keeka shook the couch pillow violently and released it. It flung to the fireplace, landing in a fiery pile with all the others. Camouflaged clothing lay strewn and blazing from the mound of incinerating fabric.

One of the walls had already caught, blazing brightly as it crept up to the second floor.

Richard smiled and looked at the mountain of furnishings piled up outside the bathroom door, admiring their handiwork.

Keeka used her teeth to drag over a flaming orange vest, laying it in such a way that the active flames licked up the side of the couch, which was now resting on its arm, holding the pile of clutter in place.

Behind them, Arnold drug Kilgore's mount over the felled pine, now serving as a welcome mat for the smoking triangle.

Once outside, he leaned it against the devastated side-by-side and looked back at the structure. All the other animals gathered around and listened to the banging of Jimmy's fist against the door and the sputtering cough he belched out before it died down into nothingness.

They all sat in brisk morning air with no sounds save for the whipping Wyoming winds that fanned the flames…

And the soothing crackle of burning wood.

52

Notches reached the rocky plateau halfway up and fell to his knees to vomit onto the plane of granite. He spun around, resting on his palms like a camo-colored crab, and locked eyes with the colossal bull.

"What is this?" Notches whispered, face twisting into a sob. He wiped the bile from his lips and tried to stand, realizing in a surreal moment of clarity that this was the spot he'd knocked Mickey out hours before the old fool died.

Part of him wanted to laugh at the thought, content that Mickey got his karmic just-desserts in the end.

But then the painful sound of the elk's bugle brought him back into the moment.

He started to rise to his feet when the elk rammed him, treating the old man's body like an abused rag doll.

***

Ryan thrust his horns into Notches's ribs, digging hard, piercing his belly with the prongs.

He wrenched his head back, freeing his antlers, and stomped backward through the dusty soil with heavy clomps.

The wind slapped again, harder now from the great height, and he had to lean to stay upright.

The bull lowered his head and bucked forward, closing his eyes so that his legs wouldn't turn to jelly near the cliff's edge.

Shiiiiiink!

Ryan's horns connected again, and Notches flinched, stuck between a perilous height, unforgiving bone and peeling velvet.

The antlers stabbed him again.

***

The bull's horns pierced his belly, causing what felt like irreparable damage to his organs. Notches groaned in agony. He latched his leathery hands onto the bull's antlers and pulled the animal closer despite the excruciating pain it caused him.

Better to be stabbed than to fall to certain death, he thought.

His breath was rattling, and a stripe of red trailed steadily from his wounds. The dry ground sucked it up like a hungry mouth.

Notches craned his neck around to see behind him and shrieked.

The howling wind swelled in a powerful gust and ripped his neon orange hat off. He watched it tumble hundreds of feet into the great, misty unknown.

He knew he would never survive if he fell from a height like this.

No one could.

They stood at the edge, jostled by the wind and the fight. The elk's hooves tried to dig in, but the surface was rock, not dirt, and he struggled for traction.

Notches thrashed again and lost his footing, yanking the elk with his weight.

"Put me down," he growled and then coughed, spattering an aerosolized mist of red across the bull's face.

The bull barked, flailing harder, but the hunter held tight.

Notches gripped the horns with white knuckles as the elk whipped his head from side to side.

One of the elk's feet slipped, and he reacted fast, trying to correct his misstep.

The hunter started to laugh, exhausted from the fight. "Your head is going on my wall."

He cackled, showing a full set of bloody teeth.

***

Ryan thought about his father being used for decoration.

For *entertainment*.

His father meant *nothing* to the man.

Just another *conquest*. A spectacle to *gawk* at.

One with wide, unblinking eyes that could never sleep. He could never eternally rest.

Ryan craned his neck upright, dragging the man as high into the air as his strong neck would allow, and flung him down with all his might at the canyon below.

He heard the bones of the hunter's shins connect with the face of the rock and the pained sound of his voice howling out.

But still, the man hung on.

Just then, he heard something.

Behind him.

Panting.

Then a *snarl*.

Ryan whipped his head and looked behind him as the hunter clambered to his feet. The man's soles slipped on garnet spatter on the rock face.

Ryan's eyes welled with tears of uncertainty when he saw a wolfdog with the red bandanna standing behind him, teeth bared.

Ryan looked back at her, terrified. He knew her loyalty was to the human.

His hind legs trembled at the thought of her sinking her sharp fangs into them. His trembling grew worse as her growls grew louder and more guttural.

Ryan's tremoring foot slipped again, and he scrambled backward in a flurry, narrowly making it back onto the ridge with the two hundred pounds of weight dragging him forward.

"Don't be afraid," Keeka muttered, drawing her icy blue eyes to meet Ryan's. "I've come to help."

Ryan swallowed hard.

"Back up."

"If I do, he'll just--"

"Back up!" She barked. "Trust me!"

***

"Keeka? Is that *you*?" Notches choked, fluid reversing out of the corner of his mouth.

He tried to smile but winced visibly instead. "Come here, girl! Come on!"

Keeka snarled, intense eyes locked on their intended target.

She lowered her head, hackles raised, paws gripping the stone.

She watched Notches plant his feet and try to wrench his body off the elk's rack.

At that moment, as she watched the old man squirm and curse, she thought about how, while she had been raised by the humans, it was the wild animals she'd met out here in the wilderness who seemed to have real heart.

Though she had always believed herself to be nothing but a pet, she realized right then…

She, too, was *truly wild.*

She snapped forward. Like a loosed arrow, the wolfdog bounded across the ridge and leaped with full force at her master, sinking her maw of bared teeth into his neon-orange vest and the soft flesh of his injured abdomen that lay beneath.

The surge of pain made Notches release one of his hands from the antlers, and Ryan's head whipped at an angle from the uneven weight distribution.

The rapid motion made the human's other hand slip and sent the man *and dog* careening off the ridge into the canyon from an impossible height.

53

Back in the meadow, the gathering of those that remained erupted into a gamut of emotions from cheerful celebrations to devastation and mourning.

Arnold and Wesley joyfully joined the celebration, exhausted from the long trek with Kilgore's mount. They were ready to lay it to rest forever on the butte with all the other terrifying trophies they'd amassed.

Ryan smiled as he saw Star and the rest of the harem approaching the meadow with the other sows and calves in tow. Edgar soared overhead, screeching the news it was safe to gather again.

But Star's face had an air of seriousness for the sorrowful mourning of Herbie, the little one the herd had lost.

"You're alive!" Tears filled her eyes. Her relief was palpable. "We saw you and that man on the ridge at the cliff's edge. Ryan, I was so scared. I saw you slip… and… we saw Keeka.."

"She *saved* me." Ryan gritted his teeth to keep from crying, feeling the pressure in his ivories.

Star nuzzled his neck momentarily, tears rolling down her face onto his dark, coarse mane.

She pulled back. "Ryan, I found out why I've been feeling awful lately."

"You did? What's wrong?" The joy of the victory drained from his face, and his eyes studied her. "Can the elders give you herbs for what is ailing you?"

"Nothing is ailing me." A smile formed on her lips. "I'm not sick."

"I… don't understand."

She couldn't contain her elation any longer.

"You're going to be a father, Ryan."

Epilogue

One Year Later...

In the months and weeks after the war, the creatures of the Great Timbers spoke of that day in reverent and joyous tones, quietly celebrating the victory respectfully in their tree-houses and tunneled homes.

Arnold and Wesley decided to leave the Great Timbers and head back to the mountain cave from the days before they'd ever laid eyes on the Great Timbers.

It was a sad day for their friends in the forest, but the brothers decided they wanted to find a love like that of Ryan and Star or Ross and Heather and, perhaps, even have cubs of their own one day. *That* they could not do in the Great Timbers.

Edgar now wore Tom's glasses when needed; the human didn't need them anymore. In a curious experiment, Ross and Richard worked together to bend the metal ear hooks so they could be slid onto the bird, like goggles.

Edgar was able to forage for himself now and was delighted in the ability to clearly see his friends.

Kilgore's mount had been nestled in with the cache of traps and found weapons up on the butte, serving as a place to warn future young about the dangers of such intruders, just as it had been to Ryan and Edward years before.

And as for Ryan, the strong elk walked out into the meadow as he did every night.

The tall grass tickled his low, dark mane as he lay down and looked up into the sky full of shining stars.

He heard the hiss of footsteps in the grass and turned to see his calf, only a month old, walking towards him. His knees were knobby and unsteady, but watching him learn to walk gave the bull a sense of great pride, much like what his father must have felt.

The calf lay next to Ryan and looked up into the night sky. "What you looking at, dad?"

"Well, when I was a boy about your age, my father, Big Bob, told me that when those stars right there by the bright one form the shape of antlers, anything you wish for will come true."

"Does it work?"

Ryan nodded.

"What did you wish for?"

The bull sat in silence for a moment.

"I wished for a miracle." He nuzzled his snout up against his son's face and smiled. "And I got it."

As the cool summer breeze blew, warning the animals of the impending finale of summer, a voice called out from the treeline.

A loving face emerged.

"Ryan, it's past Bob's bedtime," cooed Star.

Ryan nudged his son. "You'd better get back. Mom's calling."

"Okay," he said, mouth stuffed full of writhing, green tendrils of foliage.

"Hey, don't talk with your mouth full," he chirped, but the spotted calf had already taken off running for his mother, knock-kneed and clumsy, half-galloping through the field.

Star smiled at Ryan from afar.

It had been a year since humans had come to hunt in the Great Timbers. Ryan did not doubt that there would come a time to fight again.

A time to rise up and protect their utopia.

It was a time to once again show the humans that they wouldn't be displaced and would not go gently... nor quietly.

They would no longer allow themselves to be the trophies and decorations of man.

But for now, life was peaceful again. Bonds were stronger, the society tighter.

The chittering laughter, mews, squawks, and chirps echoed warmly throughout the meadow into the night air.

Yes. Life was good again in the Great Timbers.

About the Author

James Kane is an oil field chromatographer with numerous, worldwide accolades in his field. He has owned and operated his own laboratory in Wyoming since 1984.

In his free time, James finds himself lake fishing for trout and walleye, tending plants in his greenhouse, or playing endless-Frisbee with his German Shepard, Bruno.

Want updates on any sequels or upcoming releases?
Join our mailing list at
www.rustyogrepublishing.com

<u>A Note From the Publishers:</u>

On behalf of Rusty Ogre Publishing, we would like to thank you for taking the time to read The Great Timbers by debut author, James A. Kane. Without you, there would truly be no reason for any of this to exist in the world as it does now, and for that, we thank you.

This book would not be possible without the help of several people who we would like to thank.

First and foremost, we would like to thank Rick Wohl, our consultant. Rick has been a respectful and ethical hunter for most of his life and he was a Godsend when it came to fact-checking this book and fixing plot issues that arose as Erica did the developmental edit. This book would not be what it is without him. As an added bonus, we named a beaver after him in the book after his recent, real life run-in with one of the mischievous varmints.

Speaking of edits, we also wish to thank our wonderful editor, Amanda Jean Ruzsa, who professionally proofreads all of our books before publication.

We also wish to thank Emma Sahlin who worked for days getting James's book from a photocopied word-processor copy into a digital document that Erica and Heather could edit. We really appreciate that. This would have been an impossible task, if not for you.

And to the RMEF (The Rocky Mountain Elk Foundation) whose site was referenced many, many times to ensure we have this book as close to accurate as possible.

As animal rescuers and pet owners, this story spoke to us. Though it needed a fair bit of work, we felt that the story was worth it. It had substance and meaning. It was a tale of characters you could root for and empathize with.

We want to make it clear, though, that it is not Rusty Ogre's position to demonize hunters. Though this story has a broad message that can be misinterpreted that way, we felt the Great Timbers was more about waste, greed, excess and hunters who simply kill for the trophy.

We do support ethical hunters. Not just ones who kill for food, but also the ones who do it for sport or population control as long as the animal is dispatched with the least amount of suffering possible, and that nothing goes to waste. This book, we feel, has a larger message than all of that, which is why we have added this to our release library.

Finally, we would like to ask that anyone who has read this book to please consider leaving an honest review online. Those all help us improve our visibility greatly on the internet and educate others on whether the book will be a good fit for them.

Every review helps, even if it isn't five stars. It doesn't have to be long, either! A few words will do just fine. We appreciate anything we can get as a budding publishing house. Thank you.

Sincerely,

Erica Summers & Heather Wohl
Co-Owners of Rusty Ogre Publishing

More From Rusty Ogre Publishing:

From Ashes: Book One of the Illuminator Saga By Heather Wohl

Available now in paperback, hardcover, & ebook!

Elf blacksmith, Quistix, suffers a tragic loss the night a bandit invades her humble Bellaneau home in search of "The Illuminator." After months of crushing loneliness, the disheveled half-elf is out for blood, seeking revenge on the man who shattered her once-contented life and answers about why this alleged Illuminator is so highly sought-after. A wounded wyl, a brilliant esteg, and child-like dragonling soon join her on her cross-country adventure, banding together in a riotous, misfit crew. But Destoria is a dangerous place. The isle is bursting with clever hybrid creatures, floating magical cities, bandits, and a sadistic, dikeeka-peddling new queen: Exos Tempest.

The Choice is Yours: Yakshar's Lost Treasure

By Rowen Sikora and Erica Summers

Available worldwide in paperback. Also available in ebook.

Third graders, Rowen and Ella, take you on an adventure on their homemade boat to find Yakshar's legendary lost treasure. Danger lurks around nearly every corner and only YOU can guide these third graders to the gold and riches they seek! *Yahskar's Lost Treasure* is a fun, full-color adventure where you choose your path! It features multiple endings so it can be enjoyed again and again. For fans of the *Geronimo Stilton* books or the classic *Choose Your Own Adventure* series.

Desdemona in Embers: Book Two of the Illuminator Saga by Heather Wohl

The journey continues.

Available now in paperback, hardcover, ebook, and Kindle Unlimited!

Call of the Wyl: *A Destorian Stand-Alone Fantasy Novella by Heather Wohl*

Releases January 23, 2024 in paperback, hardcover, and ebook!

The Undead Queen:
Book Three of the Illuminator Saga
by Heather Wohl

Releases Summer of 2024 in paperback, hardcover, and ebook!

The Billionaire's Assistant

By Odessa Alba

Releases March 19, 2024 in paperback, discrete hardcover, ebook, and audiobook

Welcome to Greenwich, Connecticut. Unable to don his outrageously-expensive, bespoke suits and perform everyday tasks now that he's injured, attractive billionaire, Eric, is desperate for an assistant. He hires temporary help, Kira, to run errands and help with his daughter, Bella, but the moment the wild blonde arrives, Eric's tense, cold life is completely upended. But with every caress, every stolen kiss… *they're playing with fire.*

This is book one of the New England Billionaires Series. It can be read as a standalone or as a sequential part of the series. *Guaranteed HEA & no cheating.*

BAD GOD'S TOWER

A Western Horror Novelette

By Erica Summers

Available in paperback, hardcover, e-book, & audiobook

Vicious criminals, Eugene Dempsey and Chester Craven, escape Wyoming Territorial Prison armed with nothing but striped prisoner pajamas and a Lakota's hand-drawn map that, according to legend, will lead them to unfathomable riches below Devil's Tower. With two determined buffalo soldiers nipping their heels, the sadistic escapees will soon realize all the gold in the land isn't worth what lies in wait for them in the claustrophobic underground beneath.

An Uma Blanchard Cozy Mystery

Mourning Waffles:
An Uma Blanchard Cozy Mystery (Book One)
by Trixie Fairdale

Releases Spring of 2024 in paperback, hardcover,
and ebook!